RASIKA BHAT  wedding plann... has a degree in English... are no shortcuts to hard work. And success is 80 per cent hard work and 20 per cent being at the right place at the right time.

She has worked as a visual artist and a copywriter with Archies where she first got the opportunity to showcase her creativity before starting her own wedding designing and planning company twenty years ago.

She started with a team of two talented people and slowly became a name to reckon with in the wedding industry. She has been a part of some bigwig weddings all over the country.

She also got an opportunity to take on some international projects in the UAE and South-East Asia. She feels lucky to earn a living by following her passion.

Connect with Rasika on
Website   – www.weddingcommitment.com
           www.thegrandindianchariot.com
Facebook – Rasika Bhatia and wedding commitments
Instagram – inlovewithdecorandevents

THE GREAT INDIAN TAMASHA

ADVENTURES OF A WEDDING PLANNER

Rasika Bhatia

Om Books International

First published in 2023 by

Om Books International

Corporate and Editorial Office
A-12, Sector 64, Noida 201 301
Uttar Pradesh, India
Phone: +91 120 477 4100
Email: editorial@ombooks.com
Website: www.ombooksinternational.com

Sales Office
107, Ansari Road, Darya Ganj,
New Delhi 110 002, India
Phone: +91 11 4000 9000
Email: sales@ombooks.com
Website: www.ombooks.com

Copyright © Rasika Bhatia 2023

The views and opinions expressed in this book are those of the author, and have been verified to the extent possible, and the publishers are in no way liable for the same. Some names have been changed to protect the identity of the persons concerned.

All rights reserved © No part of this book may be reproduced or transmitted in any form by any means, electronic or mechanical, including photocopying and recording, or by any information storage and retrieval system, except as may be expressly permitted in writing by the publisher.

ISBN: 978-93-5376-741-9

Printed in India

10 9 8 7 6 5 4 3 2 1

To

The stars of the stories inside,
these pages would not have existed if it wasn't for you

All the stories in this book are real but the names are not
So my smart readers cannot connect the dots.
The real identity of the character stays safe and sound
So as a wedding planner I can still be around.
But still if you think you have guessed it right,
Just be real quiet!
After all, it can be a coincidence,
So sit tight and enjoy the joyride!

Contents

Preface xi

1. In the Don's Den 1
2. The Chosen One 18
3. Nautanki in Real Life 24
4. The Wedding Busters 32
5. Battling Bullies and Badmash Company 37
6. Mandap of Miracle 48
7. 'I'm Going to Make You an Offer You Cannot Resist' 54
8. Finding the Sherlock Holmes in Me 59
9. Money Can't Buy You Love 67
10. When an Audi Is Not Enough 73

11. Karma Is a Bitch 80

12. Trouble in the Garden of Eden 91

13. Battling a Hostage Situation 106

14. Fault in the Stars? 114

15. How Mother Gothel Got Me Tangled 119

16. Pressing the Wrong Button 124

17. To the Rescue, à la Sholay Style 129

18. Mrs Voldemort 135

19. Tenali Rama Caught Red-handed 141

20. Guns and Roses 146

21. 'Darr Ke Aage Jeet Hai' 152

22. The Wedding Battlefield 162

Acknowledgements 167

Preface

'It's okay to let go. You can go home and sleep—it is not a crime—and let your team manage the work. Trust them.' Many a time I have been given this advice. But no, that never worked for me. I had to have my hand in the rose bucket or I had to have the golden paint on my hand to give the right brushstroke to a prop. It was all too mesmerizing for me—the whiff of paint and flowers, the aroma of hot samosas from the lousiest stand in the greasiest paper bag possible, but in the do-or-die situation we land up in when at work, even that tasted like food fit for the gods. Only the first few sips of the cutting chai I have on the sets could recharge me. In the chilly mornings when we leave for a site, ours would often be the only car on the road with the heater on full blast. Soon we would get down on the battleground, defying time, sleep, weather, and human endurance. Being a wedding planner can prepare you for anything in life. Just as if you can drive in Delhi, you can drive anywhere in the world. I feel if you can organize successful events, there is no Herculean task left for you to test your ability with. You have to build Rome every day and you do not have centuries, just insane deadlines.

I learnt this very late, after fifteen years, but better late than never! Trust your team; after all, you trained them well. I take pride in the fact that I managed to 'possess' their minds (in a good way), worked on them till they became a version of me with the same madness and passion I have running in my blood and no longer considered it a job but a religion. That is when I decided I could 'go home' for a bit.

Whenever my husband, Yash, and I would go out to meet our friends, they would ask us how everything was going. We would always have plenty of anecdotes to tell and be witness to their peals of laughter or disbelief. Yash and I are often called Bittoo and Shruti from the famous Bollywood movie *Band Baaja Baaraat*, though I never liked that reference.

This book is based on my lived experience and is not a fiction. I want to thank all my clients for teaching me valuable life's lessons because they helped me grow wiser. The experiences I have gone through are hilarious and dazzling, sprinkled with some heartbreaking and sad moments. I would jot them down in a journal but not seriously, until I came back from a site one night. Shocked at what I had witnessed, I picked up my pen—or should I say my Blackberry phone—on which I started typing out at 1 a.m. on 19 July 2011.

I must tell you who I am. I am a dreamer. Every wedding I do becomes my event. I become possessive about it like a baby every time. Being a wedding planner provides me with the wonderful opportunity to give shape to my clients' imagination and turn their dreams into reality right in front of their eyes. I am passionate about my work. I am a party planner, wedding decorator, and as some like to put it, a 'tentwali' too. Turning special moments into lifelong memories is my job and, boy, do I love it! Understanding the clients' needs and desires and giving them hope and reassurance make you a do-gooder too. Very few people are lucky enough to do what they love doing professionally. I have loved it, lived it, breathed it.

This book is also a chronicle of my mistakes and a handbook of some must-know facts for any person embarking on a journey as an event manager, of how to be wary of the wolves in the trade who are out there just to take away your profits.

I invite you to a breathtaking journey with me as I reveal what is behind the scenes of a glamorous Indian wedding.

1

In the Don's Den

'Trust me! Trust me!' The father said.
It brings tears of laughter to my eyes every time I think about the experience.

The First Meeting

I got ready with my laptop and folders in place. I wore my good trousers and a clean, red-and-black chequered shirt. It was the wedding of an NRI girl who had come to India to marry her fiancé. I reached the house in the posh locality of Greater Kailash-II in New Delhi with my colleague, Kanchan. We got down from the car and rang the bell. Little did we know that we would be ringing the bell of that house for the next two years!

The call was answered by a few regular questions: 'Who are you? Where have you come from?' I answered, 'I'm here to meet Mr Surana.'

A gruff morning voice, which gave the impression that the person it belonged to had not even had his morning tea, yelled at the poor guy who answered the door, 'Let them in, I know who they are!' As I heard the voice and started walking in, I imagined a grumpy man in shorts and T-shirt, unshaven face, and uncombed hair. I entered the living room and saw *exactly* that. His eyes were half-closed as if his hangover had not left him. He beckoned us to have a seat. We did so as we wished him good morning. He sipped his tea and started talking immediately. 'So, let's see your work.' Out of practice, we gave our visiting cards to the man for whom bending forward to take them was also a task. After the initial exchange of words, we began our meeting. We asked about the bride and how he got our reference.

He pulled the curtains away and pointed outside at the house in the opposite lane. 'You did a wedding for the people across the road?'

I said, 'Yeah, we did.'

'So, I attended all the functions and took your contact number from him. My taste and standard are way above his, though.'

I thought, *Yes, right. I can see that.* The interiors of the house seemed rather new; maybe he was nouveau riche but he had a fully loaded bar with the most expensive scotch and single malts, which made me think, *Well, at least he can spend.* I pulled the reins on my thoughts and got back to concentrating on what I had to deal with the man sitting in front of me. My colleague took details of the dates and functions and was ready to begin her presentation.

I said, 'That's great, Mr Surana. The Grover family across the lane were very happy with the set-ups. So, let's show you what all we do.' And the presentation started. Precisely two minutes later, a woman walked in who looked like his female version. We figured she must be his sister.

The so far not-so-excited client suddenly burst into life and said, 'Good morning, my sweet little baby!' I wondered where the heck the 'little baby' was and started looking around. Kanchan tugged at my shirt as though asking me to control myself. 'So, girls, meet the bride, Ramita!'

I gagged for a second but composed myself instantly and jumped to my feet with a broad, fake smile. 'Hello! Congratulations to you, and good morning. We are here, so now you can leave all your work to us and catch up on your sleep as much as you can because, honey, you need to look as radiant as you look today on your D-Day, which is just two months away!'

I could swear I saw the bride-to-be blush as she plunked herself right next to me and started on her dream revelation. It is part of my trade where we hear how the bride has dreamt of the moment when she will be getting married and how perfect and fairy-tale-like it has to be. We tried to understand her vision. I tried very hard to listen because I needed coffee, but two words from her mouth brought me back to the present and I looked up in horror. *Her dream will be my nightmare*, I thought. I felt rudely pulled out of my reverie.

She wanted to come down from the moon to the wedding stage! Under normal circumstances, it is nothing. You have a hydraulic lift system in which the person can go up to a great height and come down smoothly. It is a heavy-duty structure that can take any amount of weight like an elevator.

But this bride wanted to walk step by step down a magical staircase out of nowhere, she wanted to climb down a stairwell from the moon with a focus light on her face. She wanted a delicate, transparent, framed staircase to be built for her with wire mesh so that her outfit—the traditional wedding lehenga—was not hidden in the process. That also I could understand. The hard part that I could not wrap my head around was that she seemed to weigh 150 kg. The outfit on an average weighs another 20 kg. And she did not want to use a hydraulic lift! God Almighty! What was I supposed to do? *Make a slide for her and push her down to the stage?* All kinds of thoughts crossed my mind, searching for an answer. What the hell was I supposed to say? I heard myself saying, 'Okay, can be done.' I looked at Kanchan, whose mouth was open and eyes even wider, and I gestured to her to close it.

'Well, Ramita,' I said to the bride, 'I'm sure it's not impossible but I must tell you there is a little risk involved as you don't want to use the hydraulic lift and this makes the whole process manual and laborious, for you especially, with the 50-kg-load of the lehenga that you are describing to me.'

The bride said, 'Yes! My lehenga is being made in Jaipur and it has gemstones. *Big, big* gemstones!' She screamed. *Everything was out-of-the ordinary here.* I wondered if there was anything normal about the meeting.

'That's my problem. I will come down anyhow. I'm confident!' She exclaimed and started jumping. I wanted to ask, 'And how confident are you about losing weight?'

We moved on to discussing the other aspects of the wedding but my mind was still wondering how I would get her down the stairs. Roll her off like a snowball? Or better still, I could put that emergency aircraft rescue slide for her to come down.

We discussed the events, the decor, the entertainment, and finally a rough draft of the schedule and things-to-do list was ready by the end of three hours. Tasteless white coffee was served in between. It was coffee only nominally; it was more like a cup of full-cream milk with a pinch of coffee powder. We packed up and left after a while.

The next meeting went on as planned with no idea of how she was going to come down from the moon, but she had my assurance that we would do it. With contracts signed and sealed, we were hired as the event planners of Ramita. We received our first cheque, after which we usually start the preparations.

At the back-end office, the production team—headed by my husband—was in discussions over the weight of the bride in full swing. We called an architect and a friend who made flyovers for the Delhi government to help us plan. Diagrams were made, AutoCAD presentations were prepared. We now had the actual distance the bride would travel on foot, coming down with each step as she would approach the stage—a 20-metre descent and over 100 steps to be climbed down with a support after every 3 metres—but the catch was the delicate framework of the structure, which the bride insisted on to climb down from. Ugh!

We explained to our clients the draft and diagram of the descent, the cost implications, and everything else to do with the plan. This cost was not included in the contract as we were trying to figure out how we would make it in the first place. The production team got ready, the welding unit was in place, the heavy-duty iron pillars in various dimensions were off-loaded at our godown, and a team of sixteen welders and twenty helpers got on to making the 'moon walk'. Meanwhile, our meetings matured to the next level of assembling colour swatches for the themes.

The Preparations

The cocktail party had a heady Punjab theme—we had women coming from Amritsar to cook various delicacies of Punjab; phulkari was used extravagantly on the upholstery. The set-up of the event was in the front of his farmhouse. The road was blocked for two days to put up the structures. The interiors were done with mud work, also known as *chowkpoorna*, on the walls with mirrors embedded in the wet mud so that they stuck immediately; beautiful motifs were formed on the walls; the ceiling was colourfully draped in yellow, orange, fuchsia, and green fabrics; and charpoys were woven in colourful threads for the seating.

Bangle-makers, mehndi artists, hair stylists were arranged for the women. For the men, hookahs were placed along the charpoys. A *jootiwala* was also there to give *jooti*s to all the guests, based on their choice and size.

Well, all I can say is that the client went all out for the arrangements, but the constant feeling of unrest did not leave me whenever I dealt with Mr Surana.

Night before the Descent

We were at the venue—the farm where the grand cocktails were going to take place—and we were setting it up. The giant staircase had been shipped to the venue from the workshop during the day, so that was in order; the assembling of the same was in full swing. It was like a scene out of *Gulliver's Travels*. The workers looked like the Lilliputians moving, pushing, lifting it all up at the same time, trying to get it in the right position. Over a hundred men just for labour and a few supervisors were assigned the job of lifting it to the right position, after which the welding unit would weld it to the frame that would make the descent design. (Later, this staircase would be cut into pieces and used in various houses for people to go from the ground floor to the terrace.)

By the crack of dawn, it was almost finished, and as the sun rose, it looked as if it was rising especially for us and shining even brighter. The morning rays made the structure look so magnificent and royal that it looked fit enough for gods and goddesses to descend.

It was the first time my contract included the clause: any accident was not my responsibility as the client was taking the risk of her own accord. She signed it without even reading it. After this experience, we added clauses like rain, fire, earthquakes, internal family disagreements, or even breaking of the marriage at the last minute—you jolly well pay up, my devils!

Tonight Is the Night

The fabrics were swaying in the air, the theme being 'colours of life'. It was really looking vibrant and lively. The furniture was all set, the layout was perfect, the scene inside the dinner tent looked like a carnival, and the stage for the couple was bestowed with flowers going all the way up the 30-metre railing of the staircase.

When my assistant informed me that the bride had arrived, I was under the staircase conducting my final inspections. I sprang up and made a dash for the bridal room. Just before that, I went to Yash and asked him, 'Will she make it?'

He gave me a reassuring pat and said, 'Yes, don't worry.'

I complimented the bride on how pretty she looked while what I actually wanted to see was how embellished she looked, especially with the 50-kg outfit. One look and I was reminded of Russell Crowe in *Gladiator* who simply could not walk because of the weight of the chains. I breathed in and asked Ramita how she was feeling.

'I don't know! I can't even move and the weight of the lehenga has bitten into my skin and it's hurting!' There was nothing that I could do about it. She was a bundle of nerves. Whatever happened to the confident bride?

It was time to wear my counsellor's hat, hence I said, 'So, is the princess ready for her descent from the moon? Do you want some Vaseline put where it hurts on your waist?'

She said, 'No, I can't move it; the whole outfit will fall. Oh god! Do I really have to do this?'

That left me in a tizzy and I wanted to say, *You gave me sleepless nights for the magical staircase. Now you jolly well climb down from it!*

After all that we had done, after all the days of hard labour of making the staircase ... uugghh!

I said, 'Of course, it will be a cakewalk. Just do as I say, honey.' I was confident that the staircase would not move, but what if she fell? What would I do? We could hear cars pulling in and that marked the entry of the groom and the band started blaring its trumpets. Shit! The groom and his side of the family had arrived. Bloody dying to take the BMW standing outside! Couldn't they be a little late? It would take us at least twenty minutes to make her reach the top of the staircase.

So, I told her, 'Alright, on your feet and follow me.'

The shaky bride got up and with the help of her friends, she started following me step by step to the hydraulic lift that would take her 30 metres up to the top of the staircase. We had made her entry from the bridal room in such a way that she would start going up in a concealed manner and reach the top of the stairs without anybody noticing her, and when she did reach there, the big spotlight would come on.

She started climbing up in the lift and reached the top. That was easy. She was squealing with delight and was happy at her achievement. And then she looked down at the descending side and said, 'Oh my god! I can't do it. This is too high!'

I was ready to push her down the steps but with great composure, I replied, clenching my jaw, 'Ramita, it's lower than the moon. Also, I will be right in front of you, bending down so that I don't come in the way of the cameras and it's just you. Just start climbing down one step at a time. Just look at the next step, not the whole stairwell.'

She backed off and said, 'No way! I'm not doing it! It's not happening!'

I was now ready to burst and I said, 'You will have to do it, there is no way out. This is the only way to your to-be husband who is now stationed at the bottom of the staircase!'

She started crying. 'No, no, no. I will not,' she said. 'I have blundered by letting you do this. I am sorry. Please let's go down. Let me go.'

I beckoned to my staff to make a ring around her so that she does not fall while creating a scene standing on the first step. I told her one step at a time and it would be over before she knew it.

'Your make-up is getting washed. Stop crying and do as I say.' The spotlight guy had been told to play with the spotlight for a while as the bride had lost her equilibrium at the moment. '*Stop crying!*' I had to yell at her to shake her off her cold feet. I tugged her hand and made her come down

one step. On our cue, the light shone on her face and the crowd started cheering. Little did they know what was going on up there. I said, 'Look, everybody is waiting for you.'

She started stepping down. The weight was killing her and, as the last straw, she said, 'I'm dizzy.' Holy shit! I beckoned for the spotlight to switch off. My assistant ran down and emerged after five minutes with a lemon drink. She drank it and started staggering and closed her eyes and said the magical words, 'I'm not looking. Help me go down, Rasika. Hold my hand.'

It was not part of the contract for me to bring the bride down. I prayed to God for help and said to her, 'Now, you listen to me. Do you love him?'

She said yes.

'Do you love him enough to climb down?'

She again said yes.

'Look at him. He's wondering what's wrong with you, maybe you've changed your mind. Look at him looking up. He's waiting.' With these words, she opened her eyes. They were very pretty eyes, and her face was like a doll's.

I said, 'Okay, then. Let's do it.'

She said okay to me and started walking down one step, two steps, three steps … I knelt in front of her and held her lehenga's weight from the bottom and went down with her with my face towards her. The descent started, the theme music started, and she opened her eyes. I quickly glanced at Yash in case it all came crashing down, but he was transfixed on the job.

And the stairway started shaking as it could not take the weight of a shaky bride. I looked down again at what was happening. Was it going to collapse? I saw Yash beckoning to me to hurry her down. The staircase was built with very less support to keep the design like she wanted. I got to know later that there were labourers standing under the steps after every few feet with tall poles to lend extra support to the staircase. But I did not know this until we reached the ground. All I knew was that Yash would not let me fall. So, we took around ten minutes to get down very, very slowly to the impatient groom.

She descended at last and rushed to him and he hugged her (maybe for being alive and pulling off the stunt). As planned, the stage burst into the symphony band and a shower of rose petals and confetti started. Whew, we did it! I kept sitting on the steps, shaking. I looked up: *God, you really love me.* And with that, I made my silent exit. All's well that ends well.

But I swear, never again, never again, will I commit to such an impossible task! (At least, at that time, I felt this.) I went back under the staircase and heard what all had happened. The staircase had started moving and displaced itself from the latch; it had been held together for ten minutes by laborious guys who did not let it flip over or there would have been two women flying down from the moon.

The whole evening went as planned. The wedding was due the next day so we left the venue, leaving behind the managers in charge of the event, and made our way to the wedding venue to start the preparations. We had not slept or gone back home in forty-eight hours. But we love it—pushing ourselves to do things that wow our clients!

The Great Chase

The wedding went beautifully as planned and so did the grand reception where I met the mighty Mr Surana once again. He thanked me endlessly for everything and I reminded him politely that he was to hand me a cheque a day ago and he must have got busy, so he may have forgotten. I asked if he had it with him.

He said, 'Oh no! I forgot in all the hustle and bustle. Trust me! Trust me! Tomorrow morning!'

I somehow only partly believed him because 'trust me' is a red flag in our profession and told myself we would see to it in the morning. (My biggest mistake; maybe it was the fatigue.) We reached our office at our usual time the next day and everyone was chit-chatting and discussing the hilarious and not-so-hilarious parts of the Surana wedding. Around noon, we came around to fix meetings for the coming week. I did not call Surana that morning as I thought it would look impolite and considered calling early evening.

We picked up our stuff and left to meet Mr Chawla. We had a good meeting with him and we told him that we were in his neighbourhood doing the Surana wedding.

Mr Chawla gasped and said, 'Oh, so have you guys got your payments yet?'

I said, 'Oh no! It just finished yesterday, so we thought they would be resting today and will catch up with them this evening.'

But Mr Chawla's dismay and concern made me uncomfortable, so I heard myself asking, 'Was something wrong with the Surana wedding?'

He said, 'Well, I don't want to scare you but forget about your payments, however much is left of it.'

My hunch was right.

Mr Chawla continued, 'Well, the heels on your sandals will become flat taking rounds of his house but he will never pay. I wish I would've met you all earlier. I would have advised you to stay away. He's an underworld don kind of guy and the most unreliable person I know. See what you can do about it. Get a lawyer.'

Oh man, the bulldozers had gone over us! And so, with a deep stab in our heart and a bitter gulp, we got back to Mr Chawla, detailing with him, which took another forty-five minutes, and we said warm goodbyes and received best-of-lucks in return for Surana, of course, and left for the day.

I called Mr Surana's phone the moment I stepped out—no answer. I called an hour later—no answer. I called the next day—no answer. I did not go over to his house that evening as I did not want to know the truth. I was in disbelief and unwilling to accept what I had heard. I called the next evening. He answered in a painfully sick voice as if he was dying.

'Hello, my child. I'm sorry I wasn't answering your phone. I am really unwell. All the eating and drinking has aggravated my heart problem and now I am in bed. Give me a few days.'

I gave him three days and called again.

He said, 'Come over and take your payments.'

I was pleased to hear that.

I reached there with my accountant to do the billing. Mr Surana was sitting right there in his living room where I had met him first, and he handed me over a cheque after a brief conversation. It was of a few thousand pounds.

I wondered, *Pounds? What do I do with pounds?*

My accountant jumped up and said, 'We only accept cheques in rupees, not pounds. It will take two months to clear this. Plus, we would need to pay VAT and service tax, and other taxes if we accept this cheque. So, that amount has to be added in this as well.'

He said, 'I have made payments to all vendors like this. You make your calculations and tell me how much tax amount is to be added.'

My accountant did that and gave him the new amount. He cut a cheque promptly.

'Do not worry. It will clear in ten days through fast track. I will call the bank.' I had no choice but to accept it reluctantly and wait. At least he was paying.

Ten days went by and we had no response on the cheque. We called the bank and checked in Europe. The bank informed us that the account was closed a year ago and there was no other account in their bank under the name of Mr Surana. Heavens fell upon me! I called Surana's number.

It went on a long call. International, I presumed. He answered and I told him that the account did not exist. He said, 'Oh, I must have given you a cheque from an old cheque book. I'm so sorry. I am returning in two weeks, will clear it then. Trust me, trust me.'

Two weeks went by, two months went by, we did not hear from him and neither did we get through his numbers. We reached his house one day and his wife was there. I told her what had happened and she said, 'Well, I don't know anything as I live here and he lives abroad.'

Futile attempts, unclear answers, and unanswered calls led us to the end of a year and I remembered what Mr Chawla had said, that *my sandals would become flat but he wouldn't pay up*. Rightly said, Fred!

We moved on with our lives and my accountant started the legal proceedings of contacting lawyers and filing a complaint. But the wheels of justice take a lot of time in our country.

One day, the inglorious bastard called me. *What nerve!* I said, 'Mr Surana, where is my money? How can you do this?'

He said, 'Oh dear. I was hospitalised and went through surgeries and …' Blah blah blah! I did not believe a word and all I could think of was how to get my money.

'Well, okay. Now that you are here, I'm coming over for my money, sir.'

He said, 'Yes, sure. That's what I have called you for and some business as well. You know, my daughter has had a baby boy and we are planning to do a big function for him, so I want to discuss that with you.'

Is he nuts, or do I come across as the dumbest woman on this earth who is ready to get herself duped twice by the same guy? I held my ground. First, I wanted my money, then we could talk further business on new terms and conditions. He just did not believe me and went on and on about the fact that the function was in two days and that I had very little time and he was sending the money by next day, so I should start the preparations.

I thought, *I have waited one whole year. I can wait another day.* So, I waited and the day went by; nobody came with the cheque except phone calls from Surana, complaining that my trucks had not reached. I wish I could have said they would never reach him but I did not. I told him the trucks were ready to load and were leaving. He was happy and called two hours later, 'Where are the trucks?'

I said, 'Oh, they must be about to reach by now.' It had been thirty-two hours since he promised that the cheque was on the way. I know it was not and what he did not know was that the trucks were also still in my godown, and I did not give the site details to anybody. I knew he was going to trick me.

An hour later, he called again. 'The function is tomorrow and your trucks aren't here!'

I said, 'Don't worry. Trust me! Trust me! Any minute and, by the way, Mr Surana, is the cheque also on the way?'

There was silence on the other side and I heard heavy breathing. I felt he would shoot me through the phone but I did not cave in.

He said, 'Now listen. You will get your cheque after the function of my grandson and you better make proper arrangements overnight or it won't be good for you.'

With great courage, I said, 'Mr Surana, my hands are tied. I know you will never pay me. You would have if you intended to by now. Now you are threatening me. I know you are a don of some sort, but I am not scared of you. No payment, no show. Even you know nobody will do your work as they all are aware of your reputation. Only I was naive, but now I know. So, you send my cheque and I will send my truck.'

And guess what, reader?

He said, 'Okay, I'm sending you a cheque right now.'

2

The Chosen One

There was a sweet, shy gentleman who once called me home for his brother's daughter's wedding in Green Park, New Delhi. As usual, I got down from my car while juggling my bag, diary, and laptop. My trusted adorable Kanchan said, 'Relax, let me get to the gate.'

I said, 'We have never ever been so late, Kanchan. The darn traffic of Delhi! It can make anyone miss an auspicious mahurat. Poor pandits must be taking that into consideration before revealing the real time.' We chuckled our way through the long driveway and reached the door. Before I could ring the bell, the door opened and a cute, jumpy man with tomato cheeks and a wide smile opened the door. I smiled back and said, 'Good evening, Mr Jain.'

He said, 'Ah ah ah ah, wait, wait.'

My foot just stopped in mid-air and I thought there was something spilled on the floor.

He said, 'Come in with your right foot, *beta*. You have come for such an auspicious work.'

My eyes widened and I felt like Goddess Lakshmi and walked in, but err … *this goddess has come to take your wealth*, I thought. Kanchan and I exchanged looks and tried to control our laughter.

We went in and sat on the sofa. Almost immediately, we were made to get up and sit facing north-east. Mr Jain guided us, 'Here, here, sit here and the bride will sit here and I here and my brother here. *Chalo*, let's start.'

We started with the general know-how and waited for the bride, who walked in almost instantly and knew where to sit. She was quiet and not very friendly, but who cares. I was sitting in the right direction to crack this deal!

The decisions were taken swiftly and the positive energy of Mr Jain kept the meeting going strong. As we wound up, he escorted us to our car and thanked us profusely. I said, 'Thank us later, Mr Jain.'

He said, 'No, thank you, ma'am, for agreeing to our budgets. I was very scared you would say no but I had full faith.'

'Oh,' I said perplexedly, 'full faith?'

He said, 'Yes, full faith in our Panditji. He had said, "Your wedding planner will be a female and her name will start with either R or K or V."'

Wow, he gave you three options! He played it pretty safe.

***

We set out on the destined date with our whole team to Le Méridien and commenced the set-up. All went well and

everything was completed in time. The Jains were very happy but then, all of a sudden, the bride's cousin burst upon the scene.

'I told you, uncle,' she said to Mr Jain, 'I told you it's not enough, it's too simple. *Bas*, you got after the alphabet R and did not let me choose the design. See what it's looking like now.' I believed it was a fight among family members, so we moved back. But as we were retreating, she came full throttle on to us. 'What have you done? Is this what your standard is?'

I said, 'This is good, it's nice. Your uncle has made the right choice.'

The poor Mr Jain was even redder now, being insulted by his niece who was being very unreasonable. But why were we being hauled into this tamasha?

I said to her, 'Listen, we did based on our discussions and it is good. I wouldn't have given you a substandard decor. Why don't you check all the halls and see properly?'

'I *have seen*! I will make sure you pay for this.'

Oops, now she had hit a different note altogether.

Mr Jain came running to her and yelled, '*Tashi*! *Enough*! Behave yourself, this is no way to speak to them.'

Tashi went over to her dad and was successful in brainwashing him because they descended on me like a tonne of bricks, I told them, 'If you guys don't like it, it's not my fault. You should have gone with the other two alphabets. So much for following the pandit!'

Mr Jain tried to maintain peace but Tashi, it seemed, had just broken up with her boyfriend because she seemed to be on a warpath. The chaos was broken because of the *baraat*'s arrival and I heaved a sigh of relief. I took my leave from Mr Jain and he assured me that there was nothing to worry about. 'She is being ill-mannered. I will speak to them later. *Aap* please *shaadi* attend *kariye*.'

'Yeah, sure,' I said to him, and within five minutes of giving instructions for the *jai mala* and other ceremonies, I was on my way back home.

After a couple of days, my accountant informed me that they had stopped the payment of our cheque.

'What? Bloody clever bastards! Let's find that pandit and ask him what we should do.'

My accountant stared at me stone-faced.

I said, 'Okay, I'll speak to Mr Jain.'

I called him after a day or so because I just hate making these calls and Mr Jain was all apologetic and said that they were not ready to pay. I asked him if he needed more time and he said yes. 'Okay, you call me whenever you have convinced them.'

He said, 'Yes, give me a few days.'

We got busy with other events and in my heart of hearts, I knew that Mr Jain would fight for me. Fifteen days went by; the pressure from my office built up and I called him. Mr Tomato had turned into a brinjal! He said, 'It's over, nothing can be done. They are not ready.'

'Fine, Mr Jain, then let me tell the office, and now, only they will contact you, sir. It was nice knowing you, but it is very shocking. I was a bad judge of character as I only gave my time because I had faith in you.'

The office took its own course in the retrieval. Two months passed by and I almost forgot about it. One day when I was crossing the signal at Nelson Mandela Marg, my phone rang. It was an unknown number. There was a man on the other side talking very hurriedly, 'Beta, beta, where are you?'

'Who is this?' I asked.

'It's me, Mr Kabir Jain.'

'From?'

'You did my daughter's wedding in Méridien.'

'Oh, the free wedding?' I said.

'Please meet us urgently. I want to clear your dues.'

I could not say a word, I felt it was a prank call or somebody was pretending to be him. I asked, 'Where do I meet you?'

'At the Leela.'

I said, 'No, I am near Maurya Sheraton. Meet me in the lobby.' He said he would be there in thirty minutes. I told my driver, 'Chalo, let's head towards Maurya.'

I reached there and sat waiting. I took out *The Fountainhead* from my bag and started reading it to pass my time. Two pairs of shoes came and stood next to me and I looked up—it was the Jain brothers. They were holding a packet in their hands and promptly sat in front of me and began with their apology.

'We are ruined, everything is finished.'

'Our daughter has come back.'

'Panditji has said we did wrong to you on such an auspicious occasion and if you accept this, we will be relieved of our sin and our daughter will lead a happy life again and her marriage will be saved.'

Oh man, what are these people!

I asked, 'What if Panditji tells you to go and get the money back after two months? You will start hounding us again, Mr Jain. You think it's a joke?'

Mr Jain was very apologetic and said, 'We have done all the nine steps needed to reverse this calamity. Only this is left. Please accept and say you forgive us.'

I said, 'You are older than me, but yes, I forgive Tashi. Keep her out of your daughter Mitali's matters, sir.' And I accepted the packet. I did not open it, I did not see what was in it. But I felt sorry for them and after saying namaste, I left.

I hope Mitali's matter was resolved. As for the pandit, he has my blessings.

3

Nautanki in Real Life

It was a beautiful Goan celebration and preparations were on in full swing. Our trucks had off-loaded to the heavenly sands of the Goan beaches. My client was travelling with me. She had been by far one of the nicer ones and I was really fond of her.

I always travelled with my four-year-old daughter along as I did not want to leave her behind, and she was by now used to site work and meetings, so she behaved herself rather well. After all, her first flight was when she was three months old.

We reached the Leela Hotel a day before and checked in. The client's son, Abhay, and the travel agent were also travelling with us on the same flight. The rest of the day, we roamed the property, exploring different lawns for different parties going to be held there—the mehndi, the cocktail, the wedding, and some after-parties. After the exploration, we all planned to meet for dinner at a beachside restaurant.

The great review started with two bottles of Moët & Chandon Rosé. The meeting was adjourned after a few bottles of champagne and hand-tossed pizzas. People started filing out. The first was me with my daughter as I needed to tuck her in and get to the lawn in the morning to prepare for the welcome lunch and coordinate with my execution team.

The next morning, we were at the welcome desk with a Hawaiian dancer at the entrance putting shell garlands on guests who walked in. All went perfectly. The bride arrived with her family and I quickly rushed her to her room with the make-up artist, who was sitting all set with her equipment to dress her up for the lunch. So, that was one task done. I ran back to the desk and reviewed the check-ins with my team. The band was playing and everybody was treated with a glass of champagne. Soon, lunchtime approached and people started emerging from their rooms.

That was the first time the mother came to me that day, looking all dazed. 'Have you seen Abhay?'

'No. In fact, I haven't seen him since morning.'

'That's what I am wondering. Where the hell is he? He must have overdosed again last night, that son of a—' And she stopped. 'Never mind. Can you please ask your boys to hunt him down? Check all the rooms that are unoccupied, check by the beach, check in the shack where we were last night ... Can you, please?'

'You don't have to say please. Let me get on with it.'

I sent six boys from my team to look for him. They finally emerged, holding Abhay from each side, and he looked like a wreck.

I shouted at my boys, '*Are you nuts*? Why did you get him here? Quickly take him to the room and get him ready.'

They rushed him to the washroom and groomed him. He came out finally, fully awake. I had no clue till then what he was all about. I saw him being reprimanded strictly by his mother behind a pillar and I felt bad for him. Little did I know that he did not deserve my sympathy. He hung around, having a lot of Diet Coke, with glares from his mother throughout. I saw him talking to his to-be bride; at least they seemed to get along.

The mehndi ceremony was at 5 p.m. by the poolside and soon everybody retired to their rooms to get ready. That day went by swiftly and Abhay behaved himself. It was the night after the mehndi ceremony that things started taking a turn. Abhay went missing again post-midnight, and I got frantic calls from his mother. I staggered out of bed and took my aching legs over to her room. She, too, seemed tipsy but she said, 'Abhay! Find Abhay!'

I told her to please relax, that it was his wedding and it was only midnight; he must be with his friends.

'*No!*', she screamed. '*Find him*! Sorry, please, find him. His friends were not invited here for the wedding.'

I paused and asked her why. 'How will he have fun?'

'I don't want him to have fun! I want him to get fucking married! That's it!'

I found it strange and turned around to follow her order.

She called out, 'Rasika, listen, my son is into all the wrong things. Please deploy one person with him.'

Oh! I need to give him a 'wedding buddy'. Okay, I understood now, we would keep him out of harm's way. I knew just the right person. I called Yash to come and meet me in the lobby. I explained to him what had been going on.

He exclaimed, 'And you are telling me now!'

'Listen, I did not know about the drugs and alcohol. Whatever the case, we need to get this boy married and get the hell out of here! I am tired already. Should I concentrate on my set-up or should I turn into a detective?'

Yash said, 'Go and sleep. I'll handle Abhay. You just see that the work is happening properly. Go via the set-ups, please.'

We both went in different directions—I went to the lawns briefly and then straight to my room and crashed.

I was awakened again when someone rang the doorbell. My client was standing at the door, her face totally white as if she had seen a ghost. It was 3 a.m. I woke up Seta, my babysitter, and rushed out of the room. I saw that Yash was also back and was sleeping. Oh, he must have found Abhay. But then, what was Mrs Roy doing outside my room? She took me by my arm and we started walking down the corridor. She had a solid grip; I could feel her fingers curled around my upper arm like a handcuff. After the first few steps, I found my voice and asked her what had happened.

She said, 'I don't know, something is wrong. I want to go and check on my son, now, now, now!'

Was she a bloody paranoid mom or what? I knew she should not go and check on him because I had an inkling of the ongoing affair between him and the travel agent travelling with us. I knew this by the manner in which she had been talking to Abhay the whole day. They were very close and knew each other pretty well, it seemed. But I had dismissed the idea, thinking who would go around with this dazed fellow; she seemed smarter than that. I tried to brush it under the carpet by dissuading her from going to his room.

Well, she was so adamant that it had to happen. Storming down the corridors, not waiting for any golf cart, we strided towards her son's room. *Holy cow, this marriage will break! Oh god, we are in the middle of a wedding. How do I stop this woman from going to the room?* After a lot of walking down the green trails and two flights up, we reached Abhay's room. I had memorized the son's room number, but the only room number I did not remember was that of the travel agent woman.

Now, we stood right outside the son's room and I dialled the hotel to get the travel agent's room number. It was 1611 and the room I was facing was 1610. Oh no! They were in rooms next to each other! Since the cat was out of the bag, the counselling started.

I said to her, 'Okay, see, whatever it may be, we should just leave it right now. You are also a little high on champagne so we should not do anything that destroys this happy occasion.'

'*Wine! Red wine! Two bottles!*' She retorted, 'After this, I can even break this door down if he doesn't open it.'

'He might be with her right now but we can talk to him tomorrow and tell him that we know and he should stop it, so it will stop at least one heart from breaking—the bride's.'

She asked me, 'So you knew?'

Now I was stuck. I said, 'As if you didn't know, Mrs Roy! It was quite evident on the flight and at the dinner.'

She became quiet. She said, 'What do you think we should do?' She started ringing the bell of Room 1611 and said, 'If she doesn't come out of the room, that means she's in 1610, and if she's in 1610, then … then … then!'

'Maybe they are just having a drink.'

She said, 'No. *I am not a fool*! What do you think they are doing! See, she's not answering! See … see … see!' While saying this, she kept ringing the bell. The skin on her fingers was compressed with all the pressure on the bell and my mind was totally confused amidst all this. She sat down on the floor and said, 'Now what do I do? Tell me what they are doing, tell me! Tell me … tell me … tell—'

'*Yes! They are in bed together*!' I quickly added, 'Maybe.' I was aghast at the words that came out of my mouth. 'Okay? That's what you want to hear, so hear it! Yes, they might be, you know … I'm sorry, so sorry, but you just forced me to address the inevitable.'

She just froze and stopped ringing the bell.

I said, 'Okay, let's call a spade a spade; maybe they are inside together. So, let's disappear from here right now before the whole hotel knows. We'll sit in my room and talk.'

We turned and the door of 1610, the son's room, opened and he said, 'Mom, Rasika, what are you guys doing here?'

I had no words because he looked like he had not been sleeping and I could smell a strong stench of cigar coming from the room. I said bravely, 'Your mom knows everything and she's heartbroken.'

'Aah, she knew it all along. Yet she dragged me to this stupid wedding!'

And we turned around and began to leave with the mom crying and me consoling her. I strained my ears to hear a 'What are you talking about?' from the son, but nothing. I paused and turned around to see a blasted expression on his face and he narrowed his eyes and pointed his finger at me and said, 'Was it you? Did you bring her here?'

His mother turned around and yelled, '*I brought her here*! She came with me. I am not going to enter your room, son, but this wedding will happen and you will not see the face of that slut in your bedroom from tomorrow or else you will not be my son from today. Son, if you don't sober up and show up for your pheras, I will not give you one *phooti kaudi* in your virasat. Promise me that your philandering days are over and you will be a good and loyal husband. If you ruin this girl's life, I will not forgive you. *Promise me*!'

He just put his chin up, turned around, and closed the door.

'Shameless coward, he doesn't give a damn.'

She was shaking and sobbing. By now, I was half-supporting her body weight on me and helping her walk to her room and tuck her in her bed. Broken heart and red wine is a deadly combination. But how could I take her to her room without sobering her up? She was a royal mess. Crying, sobbing. I saw a strong woman crumbling. I had to put her back together.

'It's no big shit,' I said to her. 'I see this all the time, it's very common. They come around once they have the husband collar around their necks.'

She looked at me, wiped her tears, and said, 'You don't have to say this, *beta*. I'm fine, don't worry.'

I took her to the lawn and made her sit on a bench. I brought pillows from my room and made her comfortable and said to her, 'I'm going to get some black coffee. You don't move from here. I will be back in two seconds.'

I made a dash to my room, boiled water, made a cup of coffee, and rushed to her almost in no time. No words were exchanged. I just made her have the whole cup and she seemed calmer. I helped her up and gave her a hug and told her, 'We will have a great wedding. Goodnight.'

She wiped the last of her tears and we went to her room. She sat on her bed and her head fell on the pillow. I crossed my heart and put a finger on my lips and so did she—a silent vow of silence—then she closed her eyes.

4

The Wedding Busters

This story is about a client whose wedding I bowed out from and handed over to the vendors. After the wedding, he did the disappearing act. Dubious and conniving, he had it all planned in his mind. The vendors got very aggressive and in no way could be wronged when they were not at fault.

When I realized he was the master of disguise, I almost gave up. But just then, my business consultant and adviser, Yash, who could see I was living with guilt, gave me the idea of handing him over to the people he had wronged. 'Just throw him to the sharks. We will see what happens about our part but first, these guys need to get justice—the real workers.' As a matter of policy, we never give the numbers of our clients to our vendors because no interaction is required. The clients know the company they have hired and where the ice cream or the flowers are coming from is none of their concern. Clients' prime concern is *quality*.

So, finally, I made calls to all the vendors one by one, whom this slimy fellow owed money to—the shoe-rack guy, ₹36,000; the *mashalwala*, ₹40,000; the genset guy, ₹1,45,000; the *safawala*, ₹24,000; the *paanwala*, ₹22,000; the *darbans*, ₹44,000; the hostesses, ₹63,000; the *doliwalas*, six of them, ₹16,000; the *phoolwalas* (seven lakhs); the *chooriwala*, ₹24,000; the mehndiwalas, ₹56,000; valet parking guys, ₹30,000; *heaterwala*, ₹18,000. The list was endless. All those people thought that it

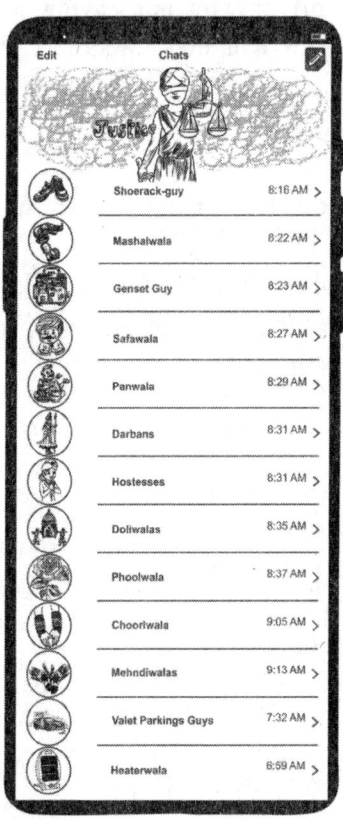

was we who were not paying them. It took us a fortnight to collect all of them together and call a meeting at our office to tell them the truth and show them our unpaid bills.

We discussed with them our plan of attack—flatten the bhatura! A WhatsApp group called Justice was quickly formed. The excited caterer said, 'We will relive the wedding. *Hum sab poori fauj ke saath jayenge,* madam (We will go with the whole army, madam).'

The plan was to do parade right outside the client's house at a stipulated time—the moment he left for his office—in full dress. The idea was for him to realize the mammoth disaster he was inviting by not paying poor people who worked hard for his daughter's wedding. The mashalwala, who was even more excited at the whole idea of a parade outside Mr Aggarwal's house, said that he would also get some friends over to create more drama.

I said, 'Sure, call Hanumanji. He will surely help us, and whoever can join in!'

The mashalwala had observed for a whole week to see what time Mr Aggarwal rolled out of his house in his Bentley. It was sharp at 11 a.m. daily.

***

Time: 10.30 a.m.
Place: Sundervan Farm
Day: Monday
Date: 17 February 2014

Two Tata Safaris full of my team of marketing managers, accountants, designers, hostesses, and various vendors reached the meeting point. So did Yash and I. The sense of doing justice prevailed in the air. I had a very good feeling about this gig we were going to pull off. I knew it might have meant running into the police, but we could explain to them. I had all email printouts and signed contracts from him.

Anyway, no police came, so the rehearsal of the 'police handling lines' was not used. The mashalwala, all dressed in Rajputana style with big moustache, went and stood outside the gate with his contemporary and lit their *mashals*. He was supposed to drop his hanky to tell us to approach.

He rang the bell and asked for Mr Aggarwal. 'Who are you?' the guard asked.

He said, '*Main toh wohi hoon jo dikh raha hoon,* sir, *par apke* sir *woh nahi hain jo dikhte hain.*' (I am exactly who I appear to be, sir, but your boss is not whom he seems to be.)

The guard returned after a few minutes and said that his boss was not at home. The mashalwala came back, so we sent the shoe-rack guy and he did the same thing—'I handled sir's shoes at the wedding. I've come to collect money for the same.'

The hostess and six or seven vendors went one by one, and each of them came back with the same reply, soon after which the gate opened at 11.05 a.m. and the mashalwala dropped the hanky. They all marched towards the gate and stood in a group right in front of his car. There were so many of us that the guard could not close the gate, and we stood with our hands joined together except my husband and me; we were positioned at the end of the group.

The designated spokesperson started off, 'Sir, please come out of the car.'

Mr Aggarwal leapt out of his car and began hurling abuses at us. They said, 'We people worked hard on your daughter's wedding. We all are carrying our bills in our pockets, all you need to do is to settle our bills one by one. So, shall we start?'

But that guy was shameless and relentless. He beckoned his guard to call the police. We were game for the police too as we had done no crime. We were just standing at the gate with unpaid bills in our hands, and my clever mashalwala who had said he would be calling his friends had a plan-B drama unfolding outside. He had called eunuchs who were dancing at the gate and the *dholwala* was beating the *dhol* right behind us. I did not know whether to laugh or cry.

At least seven cars had stopped to witness the spectacle and a few neighbours came out, inquisitive about what was going on. The other mashalwala was working at the back, relaying his sob story to a curious woman about how he had not been paid and how we were fighting for it. Mr Aggarwal fell from grace in the eyes of his domestic staff and neighbours. One look at the incoming eunuchs at the back dancing to '*Kajra re*' and making lewd gestures, and he was left with no choice but to pull out two chairs and sit with us there and then in the driveway and start discussions on pending payments.

After a short discussion and a litany of lame excuses, he paid the due amount. We accepted, we distributed, we left. Justice was delivered. I carried no bad karma from the wedding any longer. After organizing one final victory dance by the saree-clad eunuchs around Mr Aggarwal, the vendors went back happy. I am sure he will not cheat anyone any more. Otherwise, friends, you know whom to call? The Wedding Busters!

5

Battling Bullies and Badmash Company

A kind and generous gentleman happened to be the director of a very famous five-star hotel in south Delhi. He also happened to be Yash's very dear friend's father. This was in 2004–05 when we were out there establishing our business, working very hard for 16–18 hours a day. The passion to succeed was at its peak, so were at the top of our energy levels and adrenaline.

The friend's father got us on the panel of the hotel and we will always be eternally grateful to him as that was the turning point in our careers, and within a span of a few months, most of Delhi got to know about our work and calibre.

What we never told him was the hardships we were going through in that hotel to work. I was perpetually running from level S-1 to S-2 in elevators, between the office and the banquets.

False complaints and charges were made against us all the time; all we saw was ourselves paying penalties for accusations like we burnt the carpets, we tore the curtains, and—the mother of all lies—we stole the crystals from the chandeliers!

I would comply and ask my team too as well but they would just stare at me like zombies, making me feel like I was speaking Russian. They were right to get zombified as they did not do those things; we are in the business to prettify, not destroy.

I wanted to, as always, get to the bottom of things. So, I started staying back on set-ups to check de-installations. All went well, nothing was out of place. The banquet operations team was headed by one Mr Naftrat. He was a royal pain in the ass. I can not write much nasty things about him—may his soul rest in peace—but that guy gave us and our team a really hard time. Unfortunately, when he mellowed down and started behaving well, he died.

Business was getting better as the hotel's commission was being paid regularly, but a certain someone sitting in the banquet sales was not at ease; he was one of the wolves in the herd. All set-ups committed by us were criticized and condemned by him personally. Later, I discovered that the reason for his hostility was his preference for a male panellist, and that made him not only a greedy pig but also a sexist.

He would come up at the time of completion and stand with the client and pinpoint our faults. I remember clearly one occasion when we did a beautiful set-up with white hydrangeas. I had ordered a huge shipment of only pure white hydrangeas and they looked stunning, all white and green. The client arrived and was impressed till Mr Needle-Nose walked in. He started whispering in her ears and whisked her away very swiftly. She floated back as a changed person. 'So, how many hydrangeas

BATTLE ROYALE

have you put here, my dear?' I gave her some number like around 50 to 60 at one table alone. She said, 'Half of them are dead!'

I asked her, 'Which ones? Show me.'

She just walked out of the hall and did not turn back. I walked up to the troublemaker and asked him, 'What did you say to her?'

He said, 'I just showed her some of the wilted flowers and the ones which are from yesterday.'

I said, 'Wow, part-time astrologer! How do you know these are from yesterday? I have the bills to show her these are fresh flowers from today. I will produce them in front of her and please don't create problems for me. You will get the hotel's commission in any case.'

He asked, 'What about my "keep my mouth shut" commission?'

I did not understand but I did not reveal that to him. I said, 'I can meet you in your office and we can get clarity on what we are discussing here.'

He agreed, so I said, 'Twenty minutes and I will be down in your office.'

This black-suited guy with a signature one-sided combed hairstyle stuck with gloopy glue, which these guys carry, walked out grinning.

'I hate him', 'I'll kill him', I hurled so many curses at him in front of my staff that one of my artisans sitting on the floor making the arrangements said, 'Madam, *sir ko saath le ke jaana, yeh bahut harami hai* (Madam, take sir with you. That guy is a scumbag).'

I said, 'Wow, Mahadev, you understood what all I was talking!'

I called Yash and explained the scene. He said, 'Go and understand what he wants to say and then call me.'

The Meeting

God Almighty sat across the table pretending to be really busy. For all I knew, he could have been playing solitaire on his computer.

'Do you plan to work here long term or short term? I know with whose reference you have come on the panel but who stays on the panel is upon me.'

'What are you trying to say?'

He said, 'I need an income, 15 per cent of your total work done in a month for myself from you on my table on the first day of every month. Is that clear? This is apart from the hotel commission of 20 per cent which you are giving me, so that makes it 35 per cent.'

'What? Do you know how much that is? I need to pay for labour, transportation, flower purchase. You think there is so much margin? It's impossible!'

He said, 'Okay, then. Simple, this was your last event. Thank you very much.'

'I'm getting so much hostility from this hotel. I've paid so much in damages and penalties which we have not done.'

He said that the income of the engineering department and the banquet sales department did not come to him.

'Don't you guys get paid well?'

'That's a very ill-mannered question to ask.'

'But you are in such a high position. Why do you want to rob me? Please be considerate and drop your rates!'

'I am just going to drop you off the list; that's easier and faster.'

'Okay, I will send your 15 per cent every month on the first day,' and with my spirit dragging on the floor, I left his office and made my way through the long corridor, up the elevator, and to the banquet hall where my team was working. I did some calculations in my mind and figured I would be earning ₹5,000 from this set-up after all commissions, bribes, penalties, labour, purchases, etc., were paid. I started crying, I felt so bad.

Mahadev came to me again. 'I told you to take sir with you. What happened? What did he say to you?'

I said, 'Hush! Don't tell anyone that I was crying.'

He agreed. I freshened up and the Goddess Durga in me rose. Yash came up. I told him, 'I will teach him a lesson. Last time you did not let me do anything but now I will fight for justice. This is unfair.'

Yash said, 'Relax, we will talk at night. Concentrate on your work and finish it. See you later at home.'

What bullshit! Concentrate on work. I just paced in the hall thinking that I did not want to become a part of this corruption. It was unfair. I deliberated upon it for a few days. I was upset, furious, unsettled, and feeling bullied.

I was one of those girls in school who had her head on her shoulders. I had a bunch of friends whom I used to hang out with—there were five of us. Shortly after, I felt being bullied into their ways, so I walked away and never turned back. One particular incident made me take that decision to cease the friendship with them. The five of us were standing outside the principal's office in school as we had got ready to meet Mr Nelson Mandela on his visit to India. We were the selected group and the principal was supposed to approve our dresses. I wore a white shirt tucked into a long wrap-around red skirt with tiny white dots on it all over. Minutes before we were to step in for the dress approval, one of the bossy group members turned towards me and pulled out my shirt from all sides out of my skirt! Just hanging, crumpled and crushed! I was shocked and hurt and asked, 'Why the hell?'

She said, 'Now your waist doesn't look smaller than mine. There, now we look the same!'

The other girls saw it but nobody stood up against her. Holding back my tears, I tried to salvage my dress by trying to stuff the shirt in from the top.

But the finishing never came. Next minute we were in the principal's room and she looked down at us, approving all dresses except mine, and said, 'Dear, you can go in the school uniform to represent the school; rest all can be in these costumes. You will represent the school, Rasika!' And that is how the tables turned. Even if someone walks all over you, there is always a chance to rise.

That was the day I decided I did not want to be friends with them for the rest of my life. It was the final semester. We were to pass out that year, so I stayed away, talked with and met them a little less, and bang! The moment school finished, I cut the rope. I never turned back and met those bullies again.

Meeting with the F&B Director

So, what could we do with this big boss of the hotel? After a few days of deliberation, I thought to meet the F&B director of the hotel and tell him how his senior managers were treating the panellists. I contacted him and set up the meeting with absolutely high hopes and conviction that this was the right way. Turned out the wrong way.

When I told him the whole story and he said, 'Oh, he is so stupid. This is no way to ask for money from your vendors, there is a proper way and channel to go about it. He should have gone through me. These talks are not done in hotel premises. There is a very nice coffee shop outside and we can sit there and discuss what can be a mutually beneficial understanding between us.'

I nodded and followed him to the coffee shop. He said, 'You know, I have a German wife and she has huge expectations from me. I really don't want to do this to a start-up company, but I have my wife and kids to look after. So, what we will do is—you don't pay the banquet manager and me separately. You pay us a total of 25 per cent extra and we will divide it.'

So, the bar went up to 45 per cent commission from 35 per cent. Wow!

He said, 'I will need one lakh upfront by evening, so I will consider the deal is set between us.'

I had no words. I said, 'I don't have that much money, sir. I have just started my work. I came to you to help me but I don't think you are helping me. I cannot afford a 35 per cent commission and you have made it 45?'

He said, 'Okay, if it doesn't suit you, you walk away. Go, it's okay. Try another place. Maybe they are taking less commissions.'

I asked for a few days to discuss at home and get back. By now, I had a very bad taste in my mouth about this hotel, so I decided to take it all the way up. Cancel the contract! I wanted to see what the owner thought about corrupt, dirty people he had in such top positions. What was with this goddamned culture of this industry? Was it like this all the way?

Meeting the *Hotelwala*

I called the reception and fixed an appointment with the owner of the hotel, telling them who I was and stating the purpose as 'a disappointed vendor on your panel'. After a few days, I got a call back and a time and date fixed for the meeting.

I reached the floor where the offices of the owner, CEO, and COO were. It was the first time I had gone to that floor as the access was through a series of calls and then they let you in. And frankly, I never had the reason to enter here before.

I reached the office where the PA to the owner made me wait a bit. Then I was escorted into the large room. There was a big, almost 6-metre wide, semi-circular table in dark teakwood and a large chair behind it. Sitting on the chair was a small man in a white shirt with a full black head—I am sure it was coloured. His face was wrinkled. In a few seconds, I realized that the room smelled of cigar smoke. Anyway, I put my best foot forward and introduced myself to Mr SS.

'What is it that my hotel couldn't handle that you had to do these efforts to meet me?'

'Yes, it was definitely something for which I had to meet you, sir. The thing is …'

And I recounted the entire story of how I got into the panel and banquet operations trouble, the banquet sales trouble, the F&B director's trouble, and the level of corruption, and how was a person supposed to survive this crusade!

Hmm, nod, nod, nod (with little or no surprise). He said, 'See, *beta*, I'm going to be very honest. You see this? This is an oxygen cylinder.'

I got around the table and saw it.

'This is the mask, this is my life. I am a heart patient. After what you have told me, either I can blow my top and get a heart attack and die, or I can just close my eyes and pretend I heard nothing.'

I looked at him eagerly for his decision and reaction.

He said, 'I will talk to my son and see what can be done. And by the way, do those people know you have come to me?'

I said, 'No, I told nobody.'

He said, 'Good,' and I took his leave wondering how a room could have an oxygen cylinder and smell of cigar smoke at the same time.

I went back home only to return to the hotel a few days later for an event, and as I stepped into the lobby, I bumped into one of the sales team staff.

She said, 'Hey! Everybody knows you went to the boss.'

I went up the elevator to the ballroom for my routine check. In a few minutes, the operations team guy came to me. 'Did you hear?'

'What?'

'Somebody complained about the banquets head and the F&B director!'

'Oh really? That's good, high time somebody should have.'

He grinned, showed a thumbs up, and left.

I met a few more. One of them said, 'So I guess there is a flipside to everything. Somebody complained, you know?'

I would either respond or just shrug it off. I ran to the loo and thought, *Oh shit! Oh shit! How does everybody know? Now I have to be really, really bold as I'm sure those two must be looking for me with a dagger.*

I went to the reception of the SS office and asked his PA how everyone knew I had been there to meet him. The PA laughed and said, 'You called the reception to fix the appointment. The call was transferred to me. Had you called me directly, your secret would have been a secret.'

So, the receptionist told her friend and her friend told her friend in banquet sales, and they put two and two together when some high-positioned people were summoned to the chairman's office soon after my visit.

The chairman did his job. I worked blissfully for a few more months. Soon, he got very sick and retired. He stayed home and the wolves came out of the woods. They made sure we got no business, they called and threatened that they would make sure we got no work anywhere. I stepped down of my own accord and let go of the hotel happily. And as they say, if one door closes, many open. Look ahead and go on.

***

I must thank the GM of the hotel who on various occasions let me work in that hotel on special requests. He was a thorough gentleman from Australia, such a kind soul. During these years, whatever work I had taken up in that hotel because our old clients insisted on our services, he allowed me every time I approached.

6

Mandap of Miracle

The happiest, bubbliest, chirpiest bride I ever met was so full of life that the whole room would burst into life upon her entrance. She was an example of how one can always stay happy whether or not one has a reason.

She was so sorted that upon our first meeting, she handed me a file, asked me to take it back home to study, and then meet her and her family in a couple of days to take things forward. Our first meeting was all about *gupshup* and getting to know each other. I had never experienced such a loving, humble family in my entire career until then.

They were so interested in my life—how I started my career, how I got married, how I met my husband ... I learnt she was an architect. Lovely, that explained the file. Her brother, father, and mother were an integral part of the meeting, and they all were harmoniously gelled with each other mentally. One person would often complete the other person's statements. So cordial, so happy, so positive. I loved being associated with this family.

The main wedding was finalised as polychromatic. The mehndi ceremony was to have shades of orange—from raw mango to darker yellow, almost mustardy orange, from sunset to dusk to dark orange. We ended up naming the set-up Haldi Kumkum. The cocktail was themed naughty blues, with lots of shadow dancers in the background and silver disco balls.

Mind you, these were her ideas. We had six months to prepare, to create structures out of mirror for the cocktails, a lot of fabric dyeing to be done in shades of orange for the mehndi, and many variants of rainbow colours in fabrics from satin to linen to silk to chiffon for the wedding. The flowers were to be white as the wedding already was an array of colours. The bride was involved every step of the way and never ever did I have to twitch my eyelid or feel disturbed. She would take no for an answer where we felt it was not a good idea, but mostly, all was cool.

After hard labour of six months, our beautiful fabrics and props were ready to be rolled out to her farmhouse for the wedding functions. Meanwhile, at the farmhouse, an amphitheatre was constructed which looked like the Harappan excavation site as it was in levels and made with bricks. We had to do *lep* work on the bricks to give it the kutcha house finish and then completely adorned it with mirrors, something like Chokhi Dhani. That part of the farm was not to be visited during the functions as that was the *mandap*, so the jewel in the crown. The entire farm was divided into zones, with separate entrances for each function to give the guests a different vibe to the same place.

Smooth as ever went the cocktail party, smoother was the mehndi function!

I still cannot fathom how it could happen and it still is one of the biggest disasters that can happen to anyone.

As we finished our set-up, my team and I were famished. We were in this farmhouse far away in Bijwasan, New Delhi, surviving on chips and Coke only. By 5 p.m., we were parched and hungry. Soon, our driver walked in with huge brown paper bags in his hand. Totally greasy. When I opened them excitedly, the smell of samosas engulfed my nostrils.

I turned around and screamed, 'Samosas!' It was like a feast for us. We gathered round a big round table and all seven of us shared from one bag while my driver went around distributing the rest to the others. My workers, predominantly Bengalis, do not like to stay hungry on sites. They carry their ration and there is a designated site cook who sets up a makeshift kitchen and makes cauldrons full of rice and their favourite Bengali curry with vegetables. It is super spicy and absolutely delicious, but today, we could not put our butts down till five.

We all sat around the table relishing the piping hot samosas with tamarind chutney while laughing and joking, with constant glares from me to everybody so they do not drop a single crumb or a drop of the chutney on the table, as it was dinner-ready for the party.

Suddenly, out of nowhere, a few large drops of rain fell on my arm. Most of the area was waterproofed as we were in the pre-monsoon season though the arrival of monsoons had not been declared by the Met department. So, I was a bit surprised but not too worried because the waterproofing was good enough to handle a light shower.

What started as a light drizzle soon turned into full-fledged downpour, and the clouds burst open and showered every single drop they were holding. Everybody started running for cover, and within seconds, my team was on all fours trying to salvage the linen and candles from filling up with water. The entire walkway was made of over 5,000 diyas that held mustard oil. Water accumulated in the oil-soaked containers and rendered them useless; it poured and poured to no end. We faced two big risks: waterlogging and the tent giving way.

Since we were unaware of the water-holding capacity of the farm, we had assumed the water would seep in or it would flow away, but it soon started collecting around my feet and within a few minutes, my feet were submerged in water. Everyone panicked as the carpet was under one inch of water. Looking around, I saw water getting collected in puddles which became bigger and merged with the other puddles to form mini ponds, and soon there was water everywhere. There was no way people could walk in here, and the rain seemed unstoppable. Though it had been raining incessantly for two hours, the tent was holding up.

The waterproofing guy stood like a statue with both hands folded and prayed non-stop. When I went past him, he was chanting the *Hanuman Chalisa*; he must have read it 200 times but our *sankat* was far from being over.

The bigger problem was to come in half an hour when guests were meant to arrive. But how could they reach the waterproof tent?

Yash had called for two trucks of tables to create a walkway. The tables were nearly half a metre high and we had to unfold them and spread them all over the place to the best of our ability. Our team waded through water and, no kidding, it was as high as the tables by then. We nevertheless started putting upright the tables from the entrance to make a passage straight to the main tent, bypassing everything, but that was still okay. The main problem was that the waterproof tent was also a foot and a half deep in water.

In between all this mess, the bride arrived. I could not believe my eyes when I saw her come out of the car and through the water. She waded up to the table-flyover and said, 'Wow! Look, it's raining! Don't cry, it is my destiny, not your fault.'

By then, I was shedding tears of exhaustion and despair and I took the liberty to let them flow and let the rain wash them off but she saw them. I did not like this at all, it felt so unfair. It should have happened to one of the idiots who make my life hell during a set-up. Why her?

We quickly dashed from the walkway to the waterproof tent, holding her hand with a spawn of umbrellas over her. We went and stood in the waterproof tent. We all got together to discuss our options, but there was no option—the rain would not stop.

Meanwhile, at the Harappan site, a miracle was waiting to happen. Yash and Kanchan told me to follow them. I waded after them through the water and gasped. Yash, along with the team members and my Hanumanji-bhakt *tentwala*, had erected a small stage for the couple to sit. Surprisingly, the mandap area was as dry as a leaf in a desert. God Almighty had heard his prayers. Perhaps it was the waterproofing, the direction of the rain and wind, or just a pure miracle. I have no idea.

The challenge was to get the bride there. The positivity of the mandap area infused a fresh wave of life in me. I screamed, 'Call her brother. He has an SUV, so nothing will happen to the car. Just tell him to drive it straight into the waters till here, get her here. We will take her by hand the rest of the way.'

Her brother burst into the scene with his Range Rover with the bride and groom in the car. He was one step ahead of us. Soon, I saw other cars following his, ferrying people to the mandap through the tables, zigzagging around the sofas. Such amazing teamwork and solidarity from the family was totally praiseworthy. All went as planned.

It truly was the mandap of miracle.

7

'I'm Going to Make You an Offer You Cannot Resist'

A stinker of a politician wanted to sign a deal with me. His son's wedding was a big deal for us as it was a prestigious and profitable contract. This particular chap did not show his true colours till the very end. I must say, very well played.

We were really happy with the entertainment and decor and how the whole show turned out. When one of my colleagues and I met him to thank him for trusting us with such a big event, he said, 'Very well done, very well done. Meet me tomorrow in my office and we will do the accounts.' So, we planned a meeting, took flowers and cake for the honourable minister, and reached his office.

As I walked in, the door closed behind me and the manager said that he would meet us one at a time, which I found to be bizarre. When I insisted that I wanted my colleague, Prerna, with me, he reluctantly allowed us both. To be honest, I was a little scared to meet the politician alone. And that was our first red flag.

As we went in, we saw him sitting behind his desk and we handed him the gifts that we had brought. He said, 'Sit, sit.' He took out the cheque book and said, 'But what's in it for me?'

I did not understand what he meant. Perhaps he was trying to be funny, so I ignored him. He saw that we had not taken seriously what he said, so he repeated his question. When he did so, I retorted, 'Sir, it was your event and it went off beautifully. I don't quite understand what you mean.'

He got up from his chair and sat on a sofa near his desk and calmly said, 'You must be travelling a lot from city to city.'

I nodded.

'How would you like it if I said I can help you make a lot of money?'

'Yes, sir, why not! If it is something which we can handle as a company, we would gladly want to know.'

'I'm going to make you an offer you cannot resist. I have these surplus payments which need to be carried from one place to another, you know, intercity, interstate. They are in, you can say, crores. You each carry half of the cash in your luggage and our work is done!'

Oh god! I felt numb and did not know what to say, how to react, but I started gauging the distance between the desk and the door. Even if we managed to leave the room,

his goons were dotted all over the place till the exit of the building. I reluctantly turned my mind back to the current conversation and stopped mapping the escape plan in my mind for the time being.

He continued, 'On every crore, you and your team will earn 10 per cent commission.'

Was I in the middle of a sting operation?

My voice came out hoarsely, 'Wow! And how often will this be, sir?'

'Weekly, different destinations, different events. Carry different invitation cards and show them when required. Print fake cards. I can tell you many ways if you are game, my dear.'

I played along and said, 'Sounds very good, sir, but I will have to take permission from my dad.'

Did I say *Dad*? What was I thinking? It sounded silly and fake. He very well knew that no dad would permit this and no way could I go and ask my dad for such a thing. It was to be a secret operation. I felt like a schoolchild seeking permission from her parents for a school trip. I felt stupid.

He let out an evil laugh and said, '*Dad*? Who tells parents such things? Think about it!'

Gosh, he was asking us to be scamsters so openly as if it is a normal way of life. He got up and went back to his working chair. He cut our cheque for the event and pushed it towards us on the table. I took it and checked the amount; it was correct to a T. I muttered, 'I will have the receipt sent across by tomorrow, sir,' and quickly got up.

He leaned forward just as I was half-standing and said, 'Don't be a fool. You will never make so much money doing events.'

'Yeah, sure, sir. I need to ask my papa.' (Damn it, I said it again!)

He leaned back in his chair, shook his head in disgust, and breathed out something like 'Phew! Losers!', and his big tummy swelled further. I said, 'Bye, sir, thank you for the opportunity. I will surely fix an appointment with you for the same.' And then I exited. There was no way we could say no to him. He would not have let us get away if we had openly defied him.

The moment we stepped out, a security officer took our phones and asked us the code, which we diligently gave. Our phones were checked, switched off, and returned to us. We almost ran out of his office premises. Prerna and I exchanged looks and we burst out laughing when we reached my car in the parking lot. I said, '*Beta, jaan nikal gai*! (Gosh, we barely escaped!) What was that? It was like the Godfather's offer: "I'm going to make you an offer you cannot resist."

He thinks we are a gang of girls aspiring to turn into bandits.'

Prerna let out a whistle and said, 'Wow, so lucrative but so not for us, ma'am.'

I nodded in agreement.

It was a sure-shot way to make quick bucks but my values got the better of me and I am proud of that. I swore to stay away from the menacing minister and live my life with integrity and hard work. Thankfully, he did not follow up.

8

Finding the Sherlock Holmes in Me

I can say working for this event fulfilled the sleuth instinct in me. If not a wedding planner, I would have been either a private investigator or working for the CBI.

It started like any other event. It was one of those high-profile weddings where the Who's Who flocked together in the best of clothes, best of jewellery, best of cars, eating the best of food, and the best of best paraded in. Just like the Oscars.

It was an ordinary day for us, a regular, highly tense scenario where the work went on for a few days, starting from the structuring to the draping to the accessorizing. And finally on the D-Day, we were on flowers, just flowers—my favourite part of any event was when we were among the most beautiful flowers flown in from various destinations to create a magical ambience. Going early in the morning to the flower mandi and walking among the best produces from across the world is almost therapeutic. It fills me with a sense of fulfilment and positivity till one florist comes and screams in your ears, 'Madam, madam, *aaj mere se* flowers *lene ka* please, madam' (Please buy flowers from me today, madam!)!' After all the bang-bang, thuds, slams of tables, and construction at the site, this is usually my getaway during set-up days.

This wedding had a bit of a twist in it. It was already one of the most talked about weddings in the country at the time and was in a city in Chhattisgarh. We were liable for and committed to almost everything—from the decor to the coordination. The coordinating team was getting ready, checking their signals and batteries on walkie-talkies, mobile backup power banks were given out at 6 p.m. so that there was no lapse in the show from our side.

But no matter what you do, how prepared you are, you may think you have it all covered *but* you do not know what destiny has up its sleeve.

The place looked stunning, scented candles were lit, the drapes were pulled, the flowers were set, and it was time to leave finally after seventy-two hours of vigorous labour. I said my goodbyes and handed over the responsibility of the event to my management team. My best team leader, Kanchan, was on duty.

The best way to pull through these great set-ups is a twelve-hour shift system for my team where I stand like a rock with them, taking four-hour breaks and, finally, I would exit at handover time and let my team manage the show because I would be totally tired to the bones by then.

As I was walking out of the venue, calm and composed, towards my car looking forward to a watermelontini to sip in the hotel room, I saw beautiful white horses running on the road. And I thought to myself, *Oh, such gorgeous white horses! But why are they running on the road?*

Soon, I saw a few men running behind them, screaming. And then I spotted some well-dressed men running after them.

And before I could react, I heard my name bursting out of the tent walls of the venue in a panic-stricken manner. I could also hear my name being called loudly right behind me and turned around to find some stranger—of course, later I got to know he was from the family—screaming, 'Some of the horses have come loose and they have run away from the chariot and the groom is still on the chariot!'

It was all very confusing. Why the hell were these men running after the horses? Some men were screaming and running in the other direction, presumably where the groom's chariot had run off to.

I was shocked. How could that be unless somebody had stuffed a rocket in the horses' behind or burst crackers under their feet? No, no, this cannot be happening! I joined the parade running behind the horses to see which direction they were heading.

My team immediately went into damage control mode and started dialling on their phones and pressing buttons exasperatedly. Someone was calling the chariot guy, someone was calling for a driver to go around the venue, some were notifying other team members about the disaster. The groom was stranded somewhere on the chariot which hopefully had not toppled over. I wondered, *Is he trying to be a hero? Why is he so desperate to stay on that chariot? He should've jumped off maybe when he had the chance.* Maybe the horses were too fast for him to jump.

When I saw everybody running around like headless chickens, I felt like crying, saying bye-bye to my watermelontini and hot bath.

I could not find the damned chariot. Where the hell was it? Where was the groom?

A couple of my team members had the good sense to look for the groom. While I was on the main road with the team chasing the horses, I was on the phone, frantically calling a palanquin bearer who had to be around that area.

I thought the best alternative would be for the palanquin bearer to come with a group of twelve guys and we could do an old Calcutta tonga-style chariot for the groom. Or we could get a set of new horses.

My other colleague was already scouting for spare horses as it was obvious the groom had to reach the venue on a white horse—it was tradition. For that we needed the groom and the horses in place. But the groom was not in sight.

We ran and ran. It was a cold December day. And it was severely cold in Chhattisgarh. The chilly wind was hitting my face as I struggled to keep my eyes open in the glaring headlights of the cars coming towards our direction and heading for the venue of the wedding. There were political people involved in the wedding which made my heart race because I was scared about the consequences of this tamasha. At any wedding, nothing had ever gone so wrong.

The responsibility was ours. Suddenly, I spotted a shining golden ball a little high above from afar as I was running. As I went closer, it started looking like a golden umbrella and soon I found myself screaming, 'There, there, look! I think that's the toppled chariot!'

It was indeed the chariot, half-toppled, but the groom was still nowhere to be found. I looked around, and being my nosy self, I bent and squatted and looked under the chariot. There he was sitting, shivering, and crying—a frail young fellow.

'Oh my god! Are you hurt? Hi, I'm taking care of your wedding. Please come out. Don't worry!'

The horse which was still tied up to the chariot was neighing and lifting his front legs and stomping his feet repeatedly.

Shit! Either I will have broken ribs or the guy will. I wished some more people would catch up soon to help us.

To my great relief, a few people joined us, and we managed to pull him out from the side of the back wheel. Meanwhile, my team members figured out that if they straightened the chariot, the horse would be able to get up as it was the weight of the chariot tied to its reins that was not letting it get up.

As my team was busy fixing that, the groom told me his story at last. At least 2–3 kilometres back, the horses had a lightning-like attack and they picked up speed and started running madly on the road. (Usually, these chariot horses are trained to trot very slowly as they are procession horses.) The chariot bearer was a dumb guy who was bumped off within a few seconds of their flight.

The groom said, 'The reins were not in my hands, so I just held tight to the chariot and kept sitting. My whole family got left behind, and here I am.'

While hearing his story, a few familiar heads started popping up around us and a few cars reached us. Family friends, and bystanders, whom we get free in this country, made up for the baraat which we had lost.

'Why were they trying to catch the horses? Why did they leave the groom to die?' I asked these questions to the groom politely and with sensitivity, to which he replied, 'The horses are wearing my family's ancestral crest. The shields and the

velvet throw on the horses are nine generations old and are put on the horses during any wedding in the family for the past eight generations.'

Big deal! I thought.

'These are made of pure gold,' he continued, 'and jewel-encrusted velvet. Nobody ever anticipated the horses would get free and run away ... so I don't know where the horses are.'

Oh, so that is why they all went behind the horses and left him. Oh dear, money is everybody's honey!

This seemed like a police case to me now. So, suddenly I turned into Sherlock.

My team escorted the groom to the venue while I stayed by the chariot with one other team member, Rajan, trying to analyse what had happened. What made the horses go beserk?

I frantically called the chariot owner and requested him to come and help us get the toppled chariot off the road and I also enquired about the safety of the chariot driver. The owner himself was perturbed as he had not heard from his chariot driver about the accident.

Suddenly, I saw two boys on a bike lurking around, swaying their motorcycle, holding some fabric in their hands which was shining. One of the motorists was holding the reins of a horse which went across the road in the other direction and not towards the chariot. Were they thieves? Were they stealing the horses? I started screaming as everything became clear as to what had happened here.

Fortunately, a few members of my team had joined me by now. We dialled 100 and summoned the police. Meanwhile, the family was informed that we had seen some goons with their stuff turning towards the dark bend.

The groom's uncle exclaimed, 'They have gone towards Rajpal's plot. Now we should not go there alone. That is a very dangerous and notorious area of Chhattisgarh. You all also better back up. Let our men and police handle this together.'

Oh damn! There went the adventure, but we were glad the groom was safe and the wedding was still going on as per schedule. The guests were clueless about what was going on. With the groom safe and sound at the venue and the police notified, we had some respite.

Since it was a high-profile wedding, police was already there but suddenly, we saw a tight security blanket over the venue. I was glad that better sense prevailed with the groom's side and they had added security. We informed the police about the men on motorbike. We told them the bike looked like a dirt bike, not a heavy-duty motorcycle.

We were sure now that it was a heist. I was on a real goddamned adventure! The police advised us to stay out of the mess and go to the venue. We quickly left and the police Gypsy raced towards the horses' directions.

A few days later, I came to know that the chariot driver was nabbed as he was involved in the robbery. The owner of the chariot company did not charge a penny for the event and sent gifts to our office as a token of apology.

I loved playing Sherlock this time other than being a wedding planner. Which other profession can be so action-packed and thrilling?

9

Money Can't Buy You Love

It all happened many years ago when I was called for a presentation. The meeting included the bride, her parents, my colleague Kanchan and me.

The atmosphere was solemn and the parents sombre-faced. By then, I could judge the happiness metre in any meeting.

While the family was engrossed in some discussion, I started my guessing game: *Hmm, the father is definitely not happy. The mother is a no-say, the daughter and father have a great equation, and they clearly dote on each other. But if they have such a sweet relationship, why is he unhappy?* The mystery behind the glum face drove me crazy, so I asked the mother when the father got busy on a phone call and left the room. The daughter was engrossed in Kanchan's presentation.

'Aunty, I hope uncle is feeling well. We can come another day as he seems preoccupied.' Her eyes became big, then small, and she lowered them with a morose expression on her face. I thought, *Shit, I should have locked up my Sherlock.* I turned towards the bride-to-be and asked, 'Hey, something caught your fancy yet? Kanchan, don't forget to show the forbidden theme!'

The bride dived out like a mermaid and asked, 'Which forbidden theme? Show me, show me, show me naaa!'

Kanchan gave me a look which said: What the hell are you talking about? Which forbidden theme? She took me aside and lectured me on how not to fib my way through a presentation. I said in my defence that it was the only word that came to my mind as the atmosphere was so serious and Caribbean.

'Caribbean?'

'Oh, I had wanted to say Caribbean!'

'Okay, whatever. Sometimes I don't get you.'

With a laugh, I mentioned forbidden 'paisley island', so she got the cue to open the paisley design theme. She rolled her eyes and we headed back to the room to continue with our presentation.

Meanwhile, the mother of the bride, who was seated next to me, suggested, '*Beta*, you ask him yourself when he gets free, otherwise you can meet later.'

I adjusted myself and sank back into the sofa while waiting for the father. When he finally arrived, I asked him, 'Could you please give me a briefing? How do you want us to be involved and what all you want us to manage?'

He sighed and said, 'Just do as she says,' pointing at his daughter. I looked towards her and suddenly she seemed so glum. She had finalized a look and Kanchan knew what was needed, but something was seriously out of place.

We came back a few days later with some paperwork, sketches, fabric swatches, and new suggestions. This time,

the mother was not there, only the father and daughter were present. We had an exhaustive two-hour meeting. When it came to discussing finances, the father asked the daughter to take Kanchan to the next room as he had something to discuss with me. After two cups of coffee and a few cookies, I was fresh.

The father said, 'I don't know if I am doing the right thing.'

I said, 'Don't worry, we won't let you down. I can give you certain references if you want to be doubly sure about our work ...

He interrupted me and said, 'No, madam, I am not talking about you. I am talking about this marriage.' I was stunned by his confession. He continued, 'I love my daughter and today she is marrying a boy of my choice.'

'Wow, she is a good daughter. So what is the problem?' I knew there was a problem.

'She doesn't love this boy.'

'Love is a very big word, sir. She likes him enough to get married to him, right? That's why you are doing all the preparations?'

'No, she doesn't like him either.'

I stopped, put my pen down, and shut the file in my hand. 'Mr Batla, do you want to talk to me about something? Is something bothering you? The Agony Aunt in me rose to the occasion.

To my amazement, Mr Batla had tears streaming down his cheeks and he blurted, 'I am a bad father. I think my daughter is an angel. She loves somebody else and I am making her marry someone else. She went to a school of interior design and wants to marry a boy there, but he is not rich. He is from a middle-class family but she will roll in money all her life if she marries the boy I have chosen for her.'

How I hate it when marriages become transactional! So, his words alarmed me. I said, 'Now that the decision is taken, Mr Batla, why are you feeling bad? Are you feeling guilty about breaking her heart?'

Oh man! The words 'breaking her heart' hit him like an avalanche. He started howling and said, 'Yes, yes, yes! You tell me what I should do, you are also like my daughter.'

'Mr Batla, your daughter is incredible to make such a big sacrifice for you. I doubt it if I could do the same had I been in her situation. Please, sir, undo this action. You are crying just for one day, but she will cry for him her whole life.'

'But what will she wear? What will she eat? He stays in such a shabby house. He is not even of our caste.'

'Then don't cry, just go ahead with everything. Should I open the file again?'

'No, wait, tell me. What would you have done? What would your father have done?'

'My father would have left the final decision to me. I too married the guy I loved but fortunately we never faced this kind of a problem.'

'If I ask her, I know she will choose Rahul, her boyfriend.'

'Sir, how much money are you going to spend on this wedding with this *moti asami* (big fish) son-in-law of yours? You will part with money, car, jewellery, cash, property—so many things to match up to the big family you have chosen. This boy, Rahul, will not have any such expectations as he is from a humble background.' I talked about Rahul as if he was my next-door neighbour. I continued, 'After spending so much, can you be sure of her happiness? Had I been in your place, sir, I would help them start a new life together and not waste all that money. If your daughter is happy in an Alto, why are you forcing her to go in a Jaguar? They are young, they are educated, they will earn it one day.

'Mr Batla, I understand money is very important. I know love cannot fill one's stomach, but one can't stay in a loveless marriage either. This is what I feel, sir.'

I may have overstepped but I had no regrets.

'Let's do this finance bit in a day or two. I have to rework some things and make up my mind.'

With my fingers crossed and hoping for him to do the right thing, I took my leave.

Mr Batla called me a few days later asking me to visit him. I was ready with my paperwork, and so was Kanchan with her killer presentation. We made it to his house in east Delhi, an hour and a half from our office in south Delhi.

As I gingerly walked up the stairs, I felt a little lost and quiet as this meeting was a double-edged sword. I did prompt him to cut costs and do the right thing. What had he decided?

When we rang the bell, the door opened with the bride-to-be on the other side. She flung her arms around me and swayed from left to right and I understood that Mr Batla had done the right thing. After several hugs and kisses, we were greeted by a beaming Mrs and Mr Batla in a well-lit living room. The dark cloud of negativity had lifted and I felt lighter, more positive, and glad to be there.

The girl said, 'Rahul, come here. She is the one.'

***

Their wedding was a small affair and the couple, so much in love, looked awesome together. All's well that ends well!

Back in the office, Yash said teasingly, 'I heard ma'am has donated a hefty amount to the Batla wedding.'

Kanchan quipped, 'Yes, in a way, when you yourself suggest not to waste money and all your functions are reduced in number, it's the biggest form of donation.'

'Let's hope she does it only once a year or we will need a relief fund soon!'

I assured them that we had earned some hefty good karmas and exited the room. I could hear them laughing behind me.

10

When an Audi Is Not Enough

In our country, the word 'wedding' mostly spells your worth—it is the time to exhibit your riches to the world. I have seen people spend much more than they can afford; I have seen them spend lavishly just to simply show off. It is mostly a game of one-upmanship. It is sickening to me but it is my bread and butter. In my experience as a wedding planner, I have observed that marriages are mostly deals—they are business weddings, beneficial weddings, mutually acceptable weddings, my-son-is-for-50-crore weddings, and so on.

There is a popular saying in our country that a rich businessman here spends *rokada* only on his daughter's wedding and property. I have seen weddings where the parents of the bride are sometimes under so much pressure to please the groom's family that they keep drying their faces with their handkerchiefs throughout the wedding ceremonies. Why do a girl's parents have to dry their faces and wipe their sweat beads? Why not the groom's parents? That is going to be another story.

I have often seen the groom's parents belittling the bride's parents publicly. How I wish I could have told one such groom what an inflated langur-face he was, and that all I needed was a pin to burst his inflated ego. But I am a wedding planner, not a wedding counsellor.

I will now take you to this one particular wedding where the bride stood up for her parents and did exactly what every girl should do. Maybe this can inspire other brides.

The venue had a palatial stonework theme in one of the most prestigious hotels of New Delhi. I was invited to the wedding like all other weddings, and like all other weddings, I never stayed back because I needed to be home for my daughter.

It was 9 p.m. when we finally turned in the set-up as it was a tedious and heavy-duty one. The *baraat* was far back. It consisted of horses and elephants, band members, men holding huge lights, walking flame-eaters, a royal horse chariot for the groom, a moving generator to power the whole show, and a concealed mobile bar (wink-wink).

When the baraat arrived, it was time for me to disappear. I was exhausted, and just as I was wrapping my muffler and getting my jacket on, I noticed something odd. The baraatis were not dancing; they were whispering and murmuring. I said to my co-worker, 'Hey, Rajan, look at them. Such a boring and uptight baraat. Too high-handed to dance, aren't they?'

'Madam, I think the matter is something else.'

'What?'

What could it be? Look at the bloody Audi! Fully loaded with gold and silver gifts. Look at those marshals guarding it; maybe the groom's family did not know what they were getting. Soon, they would be smiling.

'Okay, Rajan, I am signing off. Make sure there are no flaws in the bridal entry, no glitches, and it should be a cakewalk.' The final words almost came like a chorus from Rajan and me. We laughed and I left, totally oblivious to the drama unfolding behind my back at the venue. My accountant, Vimal, was in the hotel as he had to collect some payments from the bride's father.

I was home and cuddling my princess and hearing her share her adventures for the day when Vimal called me and said, 'Madam, this wedding is about to break up.'

I set my daughter like a sack on my shoulder and started pacing the floor with the phone to my ear. 'Go on. What is happening? Why do you think so?'

He started giving me the eyewitness account of what he had seen and what he could guess having been said between the parties. By now, I felt that my money would get stuck in their fight. So, I told my daughter, 'Who wants to go to a hotel with Mum?'

She squealed, 'Meeeeee!'

Shailaja just loves hotels. She has sat in coffee shops for hours, digging into chocolate cake and ice cream, playing with her nanny, reading books, so I took her and her nanny with me to the hotel with the phone stuck to my ear. I picked up my driver on the way so that I could talk peacefully, and here is what had happened so far. Two groups had been formed and there were two women transferring the information from one group to another. These messengers were going back and forth, and this carried on till I reached the hotel. The situation looked crazy. What were they discussing in the eleventh hour? Man, go get married, pay us and the hotel, and be done with it!

I settled my daughter in the coffee shop with her nanny and rushed down to the banquet. Vimal was pacing the floor with his head hanging down.

'Vimal, why are you so sad? It's not your wedding that is breaking up here.'

'Madam, they are very bad, the boy's side. They are talking very badly. *Ghatiya log hain*. (Rotten people.)'

Suddenly, the music started loudly.

'Oh! You made me come back for nothing! See, all is well.'

Now I had to hang around a bit as my baby needed to enjoy her hotel visit. So, to give her some time, I started doing my checks again. I went to the *mandap* and checked the flowers and ensured that everything was in place. There was a restless feeling in me that was not letting me leave.

Slowly, people started coming into the amphitheatre we had created for the *pheras*.

I sat there on one of the steps of the amphitheatre towards the back and started taking some pictures.

Soon it was time for some pheras and the bridal entry happened as planned. The groom soon followed with great deal of drama and music and took his place next to the bride. I kept sitting at the top of the amphitheatre, taking pictures to kill time. I could see the two sets of parents sitting at the mandap. But it seemed everybody was unhappy. On my wireless, I contacted Rajan to eavesdrop on the commotion in the mandap area. Something was just not right.

I suddenly noticed both sets of parents are missing. I contacted Rajan on the wireless and asked him to find out if everything was all right. After a short while, Rajan asked me to step out. I stepped out to find groom's and bride's families standing next to the Audi.

I was shocked to find the groom's father harassing the bride's father.

He argued, 'This is not what we had asked for.'

The bride's father said, 'But the Audi has everything as we had discussed, everything. Believe me—the cash, the silver, the jewellery. Everything is there in the car, Kathpalia Sahab. You need not worry.'

'My son could have got a much prettier bride.'

I could see the bride's face had fallen. I was getting so angry; I had my mouth cupped lest I opened it.

'Please don't say such things, Mr Kathpalia. My daughter is right here. She can hear everything.'

I turned around and saw the bride standing behind me. She seemed crestfallen.

'So? She should know what big favour we have done to her and remember it all her life.'

I was now dizzy and could see my money flying far, far away from me.

'I will see to it that the pheras don't start till you complete your commitment. I asked you for something and you gave me something else!'

'It's fully loaded, Mr Kathpalia. Check it out for yourself, the PSOs are guarding it. My son is sitting with them. Let's go and check it out.'

'Yes, yes. All must be inside, I am sure. But I didn't want this Audi, I wanted an R8!'

That was it! I stared hard at the bride till her eyes met mine. We kept staring at each other for a few seconds and I pursed my lips and shook my head disapprovingly, though it was not my place to do so but I could not help it. A young girl's future was

going down the drain in front of my eyes, and I simply could not let it happen. I really, really wanted to slap that obnoxious man who was harassing the poor family. I was virtually punching him like Mary Kom and then, the unimaginable happened.

The bride took a few steps forward, overtaking me, and stood right between her father and the pig. Her friends and sisters had gathered around her by then. The groom looked up at his bride, 'Honey, what happened?'

She did not even so much as look at him. She said, 'Thank you, ex-to-be-father-in-law. If you had shown your greed later,

I would have divorced your son. So, thank you for saving me and my family the trouble.' She turned around and marched back into the lobby.

I was thrilled and smiled from ear to ear. But I quickly overcame it. *The bride is on the move, the bride is on the move, and no, she is not going to the toilet. She's walking out of her wedding!* My entire team sprang into action and we all were confused as we were not ready for this.

'What do we do? What do we do?' They frantically asked me.

'Nothing! Just don't do anything. What was done was well done!'

We stood and watched the bride go up the elevator. There was mayhem surrounding her. A few relatives were coaxing her to go back but her friends and sisters were shielding her and saying, 'No way! Priyanka!'

Bravo!

In my heart of hearts, I was torn: I was happy she did not get married into this greedy family and had saved her life. I was sad that it would be a difficult settlement of accounts.

Leaving the groom's side red-faced and gaping, Priyanka's parents also got up, joined their hands, and quickly exited the scene. I went up to the coffee shop to take a deep breath. The situation was out of our control. My daughter smiled and I smiled back. The world was changing.

11

Karma Is a Bitch

There was a time in my career when there was not much competition and the truly worthy of being in this profession were in the business. So, our company was doing well with no dearth of work, and the only dirty work required to do was pay some bribes—money to the hotel staff who would take an envelope and, voila, doors would open! We would be in the top two preferred panellists. However, this lasted from 2003 till 2009 only.

Soon, because of inflation, purchasing became more and more expensive and so did maintaining high profits. To run a business without bribing people became very difficult, but we stuck to our gut feeling and kept going on. My wonderful team worked ethically, the way it had been instilled in them right from recruitment to training. We believed in our work, we believed in our quality, and we believed we were the best.

All ethics *gaye tel lene* (flew out of the window) when the newer generation joined the business like a herd of wolves. They were more into swindling money than delivering on client's expectations. It became tough to get good recruits. I was constantly in a hiring and firing mode.

The girls and boys started jumping on to the bandwagon of weddings as event planners and managers with no strings attached. Like garage boutiques which had taken over the capital, event managers were suddenly everywhere.

I just could not bring myself to attend fancy parties to pose and have a glass of champagne with an ugly rich businessman with a 50-inch waist, sweet-talk him into giving his daughter's wedding contract to me, and sacrifice my time looking at his paan-stained teeth. A few of my friends would often say, 'You are crazy. How does it matter? You just have to sweet-talk and tolerate him. See what's at the end of the line.' But I would simply not be able to pull it off because my face is very expressive. I just cannot act.

This chapter is dedicated to a young lady from the new generation who wanted to make some quick bucks. I was in Dubai for my sister's delivery when I got a call from my friend, Reena.

'Hey Ras, how are you?'

'I'm good,' I said. I could hear a lot of background noise, so I asked her where she was.

'I'm at a party and the set-up is done by you.'

'*Me?*' I tried to recall if my team was doing any set-up that day anywhere and the answer was No. So, I asked Reena, 'Where are you and how's it?'

'You've done a very shoddy job this time, babes.'

I was taken aback. I did not take up any set-up and neither was any wedding lined up for that day. What the hell was going on?

'Can you describe the set-up? What colour is it?' I bombard Reena with questions.

'Okay, hang on. It's your signature lotus print everywhere. It's whites, pinks, greens—your signature style of flowers but not refined; your style of fabric but lousily put up. How are you going to put up a show after this?'

'Reena, didn't you hear me? There is no wedding lined up! It's June, for heaven's sake! Go to the host and ask him who's done the set-up.'

There was a long pause followed by Reena's crackling voice.

'Okay, so I've reached Akshay.' I overheard her speaking. 'Hey! What an amazing set-up! Who did it?'

Akshay replied, 'Medha. She owns a wedding decor business. Very sweet girl, fresh start-up. You must meet her.'

'Really! Very nice. Which company?'

'Wedding Commitments.'

'Reena, it's not me. Shit! What's going on?'

Reena thought quickly on her feet. 'Please, is there somebody here from Wedding Commitments whom I can meet as I want to book her for a party too. It's lovely, this whole set-up.'

I could hear Akshay call out, 'Hey, Medha!' Somebody here wants to meet you. She loves your work, sweetheart!'

'Hi, I'm Medha. How can I help you?'

I finally heard her voice.

Reena said, 'Hi, I really like your work. Where do you work?'

'Oh, I don't work anywhere. This is my own company.'

'What's the name?'

There was a pause. I then heard Medha say, 'You can remember me by my name—Medha.'

Akshay butted in and said, 'By the name of Wedding Commitments.'

This girl, Medha, was my employee. I could not believe she was double-crossing me like this!

'Oh,' said Reena, 'but last time I checked, it belonged to Rasika Bhatia? And she happens to be on the phone with me and we happen to be friends for the past twenty years and I know exactly what you are doing here, Medha. Would you like me to report you to the police or would you like to tell me what you are up to?'

Well, Reena was one firecracker.

Reena continued relentlessly, 'Tell me now! How dare you? I could hear a long pause. 'Girl, you are in deep trouble. Speak now!'

I could hear Medha's croaking voice, 'I used her name to get the work. I didn't know she would come to know, and I took her design and sent it to a local tent guy to copy because she had refused this wedding as the client's offer was low, so I thought why lose business ...' and she burst out crying.

I wanted to speak to Medha now and conveyed that to Reena. She requested Medha to step out and asked me to speak to Medha directly.

I said, 'Medha, I will take this up when I come back as I'm abroad for a happy occasion and I don't want to screw my mood because of you. Till then, Reena will see how we are going to proceed. For now, this set-up belongs to Wedding Commitments, like you have portrayed, and make sure it's a good one. If my company's image gets tarnished in any way, it will not be good for you. You can get a lawyer if you want to because I'm getting one.'

And with that I hung up.

Reena supervised all set-ups and dealings on my behalf. A team of Wedding Commitments was sent to salvage the ugly flower arrangements and shoddy fabric draping.

Medha just disappeared after that. Reena got the photographer to click a few pictures. Then she took a telephonic recording of Akshay Erani, which was funny because when I heard the voice note there was no mention of him knowing me. So technically, even the story of Wedding Commitments turning down the set-up was a lie. What Reena and I did not know was that Medha was anyway in trouble.

The builder for whom she was doing the set-up was already a part of the stinker's club of Delhi—the infamous morons whom people steer clear of. Little did Red Riding Hood know. I came back a month later and sent a legal notice to Medha and she was asked to compensate us. We were going to file a defamation suit against her as she had used our trademark set-up and brand name and presented these shoddily, which damaged our reputation. I had no plans to do any of that, but I had grand plans to scare her, which she did get.

One day, I was sitting at home and spending some quality time with my daughter when my doorbell rang. My help informed me that some Medha madam had come. I was surprised but asked her to let her in. It was her all right, in full flesh and blood.

'Wow, you have some guts, girl! What do you want?' I asked her biting into my chocolate which for some reason was tasteless now.

Medha immediately started whimpering. 'I was waiting for you to come back, Ma'am.'

I was so enraged I wanted to give her a mouthful, but there is no fun in hitting an injured being, so I asked her, 'What happened? Why are you doing this tamasha in my house?' I called my help to take my daughter to the other room and stay with her. I straightened up and yelled, 'Why did you to this? Tell me *why*?'

'I really have no answer to why I did what I did, but I must tell you I have learnt my lesson. I did it because you refused.

'Listen to me,' she pleaded. 'I took up the event but I had full intention of paying the company. The events had started when you got to know. I couldn't back out as I was in a catch-22 situation with you and them, and the money came in from them on time. I covered 50 per cent of the payables, so I thought I could pay the company's cost easily and make my profit.

'However, problems started developing very soon. My phone calls were neither answered nor returned.'

'Now do you understand what client dealing is? It's no child's play! You think he was blind? He couldn't sense what you were up to?'

'On the event, the cheque was given,' she continued. 'But how was I supposed to encash it? It was in your company's name.'

Ha! Akshay was even smarter than I had thought!

'I asked for cash but he didn't give me. He asked me to come in the morning next day. The only thing that kept bothering me was the phone call.'

'Which phone call?' I asked.

'Somebody called the office and warned not to do this event as Akshay was a fraud. But I did not care because I was also doing the wrong thing. Then the morning came and I dutifully went to his house. The tick-tock started, 9 a.m. became 3 p.m. I just kept waiting.'

'You waited for six hours?'

'The excuses started rolling in from the time I reached—the keys were left behind in the car which had gone out for work, it would return any time. By then the event was over and my position was at the receiving end and more on the edge. I called Mr Akshay Erani but he didn't answer his phone. I called repeatedly and frantically, but there was no answer.' She started sobbing again.

'I dropped SMSs stating that he should answer the calls, but he didn't. I rushed out at 3 p.m. and went to his office. He was not there either. More calls and messages went in vain. The villain finally showed up at the wedding and plunked himself down on a sofa in the hall as if nothing had happened. I went over to him and told him I wanted to speak to him as there were some issues with the payment. At this, his sloppy brother came to me and said, "What are these flowers you are using? Is this what we had selected?" I was shocked!

'I said, "Nishant, of course, this is what you selected. Here is the presentation and here is the delivery, see? They're the same!" He went quiet before saying, "The sofas seem tacky. Too fuchsia!"

'I was startled again. The Pomeranian puppy had grown teeth! I said, "Yes, it's what Enya wanted! *Fuchsia*! Look up, Nishant, it's all fuchsia! All the way!" He came up with ten more such lame complaints. The father jumped into the scene too and started complaining. It's like you have ordered an expensive meal and just because you can't pay for it, you start complaining or you have a bad intention like dropping your hair or a broken nail in the food and saying, "Oh look! Oh look!"

'The unassuming accountant reached there and told me to call you. With great difficulty, I convinced him not to and that I would handle it, and they exited! Vanished! I was in such a fix whether to remove the set-up or create a fiasco. I was damn sure by then that they were acting smart with me, but what could I do? I was already double-crossing you.

'I called Mrs Erani. She said, "Oh dear, don't worry, they are men. They are stressed and they don't have any design sense. I'm sure you are doing it wonderfully." So, I said to her,

"I'm sending you a few pictures. Please have a look and then you will believe me." I sent her the pictures and I didn't get any reply. I called her again to ask if she had checked and she said, "No, I did not. Don't worry, I'm reaching in two hours and bringing the cheque."

'I was fooled by this entire family. I felt brutalized. I felt so helpless and scared. I was heartbroken at the meanness of the human race. How did we become like this? How could I do this to you? I understood how much stress you take. I was so ignorant of how a business is managed. What was I thinking?'

I said nothing. I just looked at her from a point-blank range.

'I am sure there is karma and that whoever does bad has to pay for it before they die. Because there is no afterlife. We have to pay for it *now*, in this life. I paid for what I did instantly. Please forgive me if you can.' The sobbing continued.

I got some water for her and asked her what she did next.

'I knew I had been robbed. I have no face to show you, to the office, to our accountant who is there again and again saying, "They turned out to be fraudsters, madam. I'm going to call Rasika madam now." I told him, "I would pay for it, don't tell her. It was my responsibility." Our accountant did not know that I was doing this event without your knowledge, so he innocently wanted to inform you that this client was not paying. I would not let the company bear the price for it, and at that time it was a lie because I just did not want you to know.'

I said, 'Yes, don't rub it in, I know.'

'Two hours later, the mum, Mrs Erani, walked in wearing a diamond-studded collar, all ready for a fashion show. She looked like a Pomeranian, that woman. Though their dog is better off, at least he wags his tail.'

I laughed at her analogies and imagined this Pomeranian family fooling Medha over a very sophisticated meeting.

'She was all gaga over everything and said, "I told you it's okay, they are crazy … these men!" And she laughed and disappeared into the hall. I went to my accountant happily and told him that it was all fine, he could go and talk to her and take the cheque. He went around and found her sitting on a couch talking on the phone. I observed them from a distance.

When she acknowledged the accountant, he said, "Madam, Mr Erani was supposed to give us the cheque this morning, but I believe you have it with you?" She said, "*Badtameez*, my daughter is about to get married and you're harping on about your cheque! Can't you see I'm busy?" And she went back to yapping on the phone.

'He came back to me and told me what had happened. I went to her and sat on the couch opposite her and smiled and waited for her to get off the phone. She did get off and I told her, "Let's go for a walk through the venue." It was sprawling and spread over two lawns and four halls. We went to the ceremony area, the dinner area, the reception area, the dancing area.'

Wow, she did everything like I would do, I thought to myself.

'I took her everywhere. The venue was beautifully blanketed in flowers and lights, and believe me, she was stunned. She did not know what to say as she could not praise it openly. If she acknowledged a job well done, how would she cut the money? How would she not pay, as that was their whole plan? She just kept smiling and nodding until I said, "Where is my cheque, Mrs Erani? Can I have it now?" She said, "Tomorrow morning," and turned away and did not look back.

'The tomorrow never came. The father, brothers, mother, bride … nobody opened the doors and nobody answered the phone or replied to SMSs.'

The Modus Operandi of the Family

'The one time when the dad answered the phone was when he said, "Dare you call me again! I will make sure you never ever get any work in Delhi. I will defame you!" *I am already dead*, I thought; either you will kill me or he will.

'I thought let me sue them and I will pay you, and I confessed to my family about what I had done. I had many, many emails, so I thought I could sue. Next morning, I sat before my laptop and started looking for email conversations. I got many of the quotations mailed, presentations mailed, pictures, mood boards, Excel sheets. I forwarded all of them to Mr Kohli, the lawyer my dad had suggested. He called me in an hour saying that he needed conversations. The intention was to threaten the Eranis only.

'I said, "Yes, that's what I have sent you." He said, "Please check; you have sent me all mails sent by you to them but there is no mail that has their reply. And without their reply, there is no conversation and there is no case." I did not even realize the game they had played up until then. I was aghast!'

I thought, *Medha, your inexperience got you in this soup. Now do you realize that running a company is not the same as conducting a site?*

'I frantically looked for email conversations,' she continued. 'In junk, in trash, in my drives, in my hard drives; I got *nothing*. I thought hard about this and came to the realization that each mail was replied but with a phone call. It was a premeditated plan. I have no qualms in telling all this to you because I want you to know I tried. All my hopes of retrieval were dashed. I could have done a lot of things but I couldn't do it.'

With this, Medha's story ended. And suddenly, the decision was in my hands as to what to do.

Her dad compensated for the loss to the company, and we ended it with a warning never to cross paths again. I took a written apology in which she promised she would not represent us anywhere. With that, I closed the chapter and let her go.

12

Trouble in the Garden of Eden

Once I was called for a meeting for a Sikh wedding. The Sikhs generally have tranquil and peaceful weddings in the morning, mostly on a Sunday, followed by a lavish vegetarian spread.

One day, I received a phone call. 'Hello, is that Rasika, the wedding planner?'

It was 7.30 a.m. I stuttered a yes as I was still in bed, and my next statement would have been 'I will call you back after 9 a.m., madam,' but the volcanic eruption on the other side of the line was non-stop, and that did not give me a chance to utter a word.

'You see, you see, my Tinky is getting married. What a wonderful blessing from God! I need a venue, I need a theme which you have never done. I need the best caterer and I need the heavens and I need the earth and I need to move mountains and …' Blah-blah-blah.

I realized that I could not hang up, so I pulled myself out of the bed and walked out of the room, not wanting to disturb Yash. I went into my lawn and said, 'Very good morning, Mrs...? Can you please give me your name so I can make a note?'

'Oh, yes. Please write Tweety Lamba.' So Tweety's daughter Tinky is on the death row.

'Hello, ji. You're an early riser.'

'Oh, Rasika, I got your number at 11.30 last night and I have been waiting for the morning call. I woke my husband and daughter up and we drove to Delhi from Ludhiana. We are here at Heritage City on MG road, so now you come here quickly.'

Day 1

There was something very weirdly bubbly about her, so I fixed a meeting with the family at 9 a.m. I called my assistant to join me for the meeting. When I reached the hotel, the door was answered by someone I guessed was Tweety.

'Hi, are you Rasika?'

I said yes.

'Oh, how nice! I thought you would be late. Let's sit. And yes, now where do I begin? My daughter is getting married to one of the wealthiest and the most well-known families of New Delhi and I want their wedding to be the talk of the country.'

Well, I'd heard about town and city but this woman wanted to go national. I thought, *Okay, you queen of Punjab.* Over tea and nice cookies, we started our discussion. Or should I say, she started—blah-blah-blah ... I turned deaf while she spun her dreams in front of me about how she had fantasised about her daughter's wedding all these years and how grand and magnificent it should look and how ... whatever. I had not even opened my iPad yet to show her stuff. I thought that moment would never come.

Here was a client I categorize as 'werewolf' as they turn into designers from the moment they see us. And we are just carpenters and the execution team for them.

For the next half-hour, my assistant and I finished our tea and had plenty of cookies and were sitting totally relaxed as Tweety tweeted away. Then the unimaginable happened—she stopped talking! Bells start ringing in my ears, my eyes opened wide, and I could feel my body relaxing as peace descended on the room.

I finally asked, 'How will the ceremony area look? Can we discuss that?' By this time, we had covered only the venue which had to have a swimming pool.

'Now that you have understood my designs, you tell me how the entrance can be made stunning.'

'I am sure you must have something in mind for that too.'

'No, I'm not a designer like you, so you tell me.'

Instantly, without wasting a second, I said, 'Entry to the Garden of Eden will have flower-laden trees and maple leaves scattered all over the passage to give the effect of autumn. The carpet will be covered by maple leaves, and as the guests walk in, we will recreate sounds of breeze, and the smell of roses to touch all their five senses. Eyes will love what they see, noses will smell the fragrance of roses, ears will hear the sound of the breeze, tongue ...' (Oops, what will the tongue taste? I thought I had made a blooper but I had my smart Kanchan to complete my sentence.)

'... the tongue will get a tantalizing taste of a special chocolate offered by a beautiful hostess. She will pop it in the guest's mouth who will readily take a piece from the beautiful hand of Eve, especially Indian men!' She laughed and Tweety looked straight at Kanchan with eyes wider than golf balls. 'So, they will be touched with the whole aura of the venue in one go and the effect will be OMG!' Kanchan bravely continued to the finish line.

Tweety went nuts because she started clapping. She stood up, went to the door, and opened it. (Was she planning to show me the way out?) Instead, she went out and entered again with her eyes shut, and dramatized in front of me the whole entry sequence which we had just explained to her. She entered with an imaginary friend and she was talking to her. 'Oh my god, look at the trees, it's looking like a dreamland!' Then she turned to the imaginary Eve and popped a chocolate in her mouth and said, 'Is it orange flavour?' Satisfied with the response, Psycho Tweety walked up to me and plonked down next to me. Holy cow, and I thought I'd seen it all!

Tweety was totally unfazed at the demo she had just given us and said, 'Okay, I've felt the entrance. It's perfect.'

We had been there for two hours now. Before sharing any more ideas, I tried to bring up the topic of my fees and the cost implications of the kind of set-up she wants. 'Tweetyji, I must tell you I like your style. (Well, we all butter them a bit, don't we, when we want a golden egg?)

'I'm sure you don't want to know the costs involved yet as I feel money talks kill a designer ...'

Tweety tweeted, 'Of course not, for my daughter's wedding, money will be immaterial provided you make my dream real.'

'That's what we are here for. I loved your conviction over the phone.'

She seemed very pleased with what was being discussed. 'Well, I love it so far. So, what's next?'

We then launched on a detailed discussion about the decor and the venue.

Suddenly, a sweet-looking Sikh gentleman entered the room and quietly sat in a corner, rather the furthermost chair in the room. I wondered if I should say hello.

Tweety turned around and said, 'Oh ji, come here, you can join in now. We will tell you what all we have decided.'

The sardarji jumped up to his feet and started yelling, 'Tinky! Tinky! Come here quickly, your mum wants us to see the designs.'

In rolled Tinkerbell, fluttering all around me. 'Oh, I'm so excited! I can't wait to get married!'

And she sat next to me and said, 'Okay, show me what mum has selected.' With starry eyes, she stared at my laptop without blinking.

Mummy said, 'Now don't speak too much because what I've selected is the best and I want no changes,' and then she turned and nudged the sardar (who by now I realized was the battered husband) and said, 'You also see what you have to pay for.'

He crept up like a mouse and said, 'Okay, please show us also.'

I am sure young Tweety took the *baraat* to her husband's house, dragged him out, loaded him on a horse, and rode off.

I was at my sweetest best and gave a rundown to the other two, with non-stop add-ons and remarks by the unshuttable mother. We then came to the colours that Tinky would be wearing.

'Oh, Rasika, mum says I'm so fair I should only wear pink, shocking pink!'

'Sure,' I heard myself saying, 'of course, a shocking pink will be a wonderful contrast to the maple tree theme.'

And then, after a lot of deliberations for four-and-a-half hours, I reached the end of my marathon meeting. I had already given a vague idea of the costing of the engagement and cocktails. The poor chap could manage, 'Sounds fine.'

We left for the day to catch up with them the next day with presentations and ideas for the wedding look. I love the beauty and purity attached with a Sikh wedding; it is all about the sanctity of the wedding. (Though we make our killing in the evening and night functions which are grander and more extravagant!)

Day 2: Tweety Mania, 4 p.m.

With my staff ready with all the details and presentations, we proceeded to meet her majesty. The door was answered by her husband. I said, 'Hello, sir. How are you?'

'Oh, ho ho ho,' said the sardarji, 'welcome ji, welcome ji. We were waiting for you and we have just returned from shopping and I was preparing some chicken tikka kebabs for you.'

'Oh, that's very kind of you but I'm a vegetarian.'

'Really, how do you survive?'

'Like all the other vegetarians of the world, sir.'

The sweet sardar merrily chatted with us and showed us the way in and made us comfortable when Tweety shrieked, 'Who is it? Is Rasika here?'

He stuttered, 'Yes ... come darling, she's here.'

We were carrying some large visuals of floor plans and about a hundred shades of fabrics to select the maple leaf tones. The queen flew down the stairs and sat with us. She looked at the poor sardarji and he disappeared into the kitchen saying, 'I'll make something vegetarian.'

'Okay, so show me what all you have done, what you have got, and what all you have not been able to do.'

We said we had done it all in chorus. The response was spontaneous. Tweety thought it was rehearsed because she narrowed her eyes and piercingly looked at me. She called for Tinky and then her dad, asking him to 'go and see where she is. Is she still in bed?'

Poor sardarji went up the stairs and came back a minute later. 'Tinky's saying you have a look. Anyway, you alone will decide, so what's the point in coming down? She'd rather sleep.'

At this, Tweetyji started off, 'See? I've no help, they just leave everything to me. I'm supposed to do it all. I'm supposed to decide everything. Oh god, it's terrible to have a non-supporting family!' She looked imploringly at us but our sympathies were already with the father and the daughter.

Shortly afterwards, sardarji emerged with piping hot and delicious-looking aloo tikkis and some pakoras.

'Hehehe, please have these, all vegetarian now. I made these myself.'

Oh my! Not only did he have to look after his wife and daughter, he also had to entertain the guests. We politely took a bite or two and got on with the meeting. Madam looked intently through her diamond-studded reading glasses, liked everything, kept grinning, and finally burst into laughter which sounded like a volcanic eruption.

'God bless you! God bless my friend who gave me your contact. God bless your work and everything else.'

And I thought, *God bless the sardarji as I'm going to make a big hole in his pocket.*

She called out to her husband: 'Enough now, sit and see what they have made. You are so silly, busy making snacks when you have to see the wedding designs of your daughter.'

'But you only said—'

'Forget what I said and listen to what I'm saying now,' making sardarji eat his words. 'Now we have seen what a Garden of Eden looks like, so what we want is a demo set-up at the venue to see if this kind of look will go with the place.'

We were now ready to accept anything that came from her. We became shockproofed.

Finally, Tinky flew down the stairs and said, 'Oh, Mummy, can I have a look?'

'Yes, dear, we have finalized the Garden of Eden theme.'

'Huh, Mummy, do I look like I'm from Eden? Will my clothes be made of leaves then?'

Her mother said, 'Eden is nothing in front of you, my princess.'

Somehow, they shut the hell up. So now we set the date and time for the meeting for the mock set-up. In between they went to Milan for shopping.

At the Hotel, New Delhi, 4 p.m.

I reached the hotel with my team, skilled labour, enormous maple tree props, different shades of fabrics to adorn the walls, strings, flowers, and the works. We were at the banquet hall setting things up. Time given to Tweety was 5 p.m. because we wanted an hour to set things up. But Tweety came in just then.

'Helloo! Hahahaha! I couldn't resist coming early. I thought to myself, what the heck, let me go and see what you are doing.'

I could sense that she had a card up her sleeve, but I gave her the benefit of doubt, thinking that she had a screw loose, and let her watch the show. Not knowing that the show had just begun. My guy climbed up the ladder and pulled on the fabric in the style we wanted it draped and was fixing it in position when Tweety exclaimed, 'Eeks!'

I turned around and wondered if a mouse had come and bitten her on her bum.

'No, no, no, no, no, that's not the way I want the fabric.'

'It's not even started.'

'But I can imagine it and I have decided it won't look nice.'

'Okay, Mahadev …' My *karigar* changed it to style 2. It was also welcomed with another shriek.

'Mahadev, style 3.'

It was welcomed with a tap on my shoulder. I turned and Tweety was standing 6 inches away and said, 'May I?'

'May I what?'

'May I drape the fabric and show you?'

'Sure, why not? Be my guest.'

But what we witnessed next was straight out of a *Supergirl* episode.

Tweety went to my 4-metre-high ladder which stood like a T and started climbing it from the other side. Mahadev was blown out of his wits and started screaming to his fellow karigars, beckoning them to come and hold the ladder to balance. Tweety was unfazed and kept climbing.

Sardarji said exasperatedly, '*Hai hai, mein ki karan is jhalli da!*' (Oh god, what do I do with this crazy woman!)

I said, 'Sir, what is ma'am doing? She can have a fatal fall, I'm warning you.'

Sardarji said to Tweety, 'Oh Sweeto, *naa*. Come down, they are saying you will fall and break your bones. Then we will be planning your prayer meeting rather than our daughter's wedding. Come down this instant!'

But our Catwoman had to show me the drape. Amazingly, neither was she lightweight nor was she trained but she reached the top of the ladder. Our ladders were not very technical ones. They were made in a way that one person could climb up and down fast, tilt it, and run with it to the next spot. It was very difficult to use as the place to put your foot was a heavy cylindrical rod, not a rectangular step which could take your whole foot.

As she climbed to the top of the ladder, all my karigars made a circle around her on the ground. She coolly shook her sandals off and they fell to the floor, one hitting the head of

her husband, who exclaimed, '*Mainu te jootiya hi padni hain zindagi bhar!*' (I get shoes thrown at all my life!)

She beckoned to Mahadev to climb up from the other side with the end of the drape in his hand. Mahadev took the most difficult ten steps of his life. He reached her and handed her the drape. She held it and sat on the top of the ladder as though riding a bike, and looked down and said, 'Hold on tight.'

Now swish and swoosh, this is how it should hang. I could not take it any more, so I yelled at her, 'Ma'am, come down at once as we are sure something terrible will happen to you because it's easy to go up but very difficult to climb down. So, make your way down *now*!'

'Okay, now that you know how I want the drape, I will come down.'

The sardarji was mumbling something. I moved closer to sardarji to hear him and found him singing:

Humpty Dumpty sat on a wall
Humpty Dumpty had a great fall,
All the king's horses and all the king's men
Could not put Humpty together again!

My eyes widened. I wanted to burst into laughter and my face swelled up like a balloon as I tried to control my laughter. To our horror, Tweety shrieked and refused to come down, and she was talking non-stop.

Sardarji shouted, 'Tweety, *shut up*!'

And she did. I wondered how the sardarji had found his voice.

'Now listen, don't talk, just do as I say and you will be down on the ground safely.' She listened while he directed her. We helped a bit too and Tweety finally came down. The moment she was down, she started off.

You know what I was thinking? That this contract was going to have a line: Any damage to a person's life is not the responsibility of the company and the client will not climb walls and ladders.

After all this drama, we made our way out of the banquet with approvals on props design and 'the draping style'. The preparations went on in full swing for the event. Fabrication of massive trees to be laden with real apples and orchids to make it look like the Garden of Eden went on vigorously. Mock set-ups were done as promised to the client and approvals with minor changes were taken on paper.

The Engagement

We had been at the hotel creating magic all night and the results were stunning. The sardarji came in the morning and said, 'Hello. Wow! Looks like you have been up all night. It looks wonderful. I'm sure by evening it will look even more gorgeous. Tweety is also just on her way down.'

Oh, I see. They were staying at this hotel, so the Terrible Tweets was not far away.

Mr Lamba offered to get breakfast together. A few of us excused ourselves because of work while some from the team were famished and left with Mr Lamba. Just as they disappeared towards the coffee shop, entered Tweety.

'Oh, ho ho ho! Isn't the peach a little dark? Aren't the maple leaves a bit light in colour?'

'Good morning, ma'am. You are seeing everything without the light effects and in daytime. The look is incomplete, so I'd rather you come back around 6 p.m. to see everything.'

'Oh, no, no, no. I'm here only now.'

A buzzing sound started in my head, as if a bee had entered through my ear. I felt like snapping her head off. 'Okay, ma'am. You can come in and out as and when you like.'

'That's what I'm saying, I'm all ready and have had my breakfast. I'm not going anywhere from here. I'm here to help you.'

Shucks! *Help*! That is what I wanted to yell. God help me! She poked around the set-up the whole day. At about 4 p.m. something started happening to Tweety. One of my assistants came and told me, 'Ma'am, see what she's doing.' Out of curiosity, I searched for her in the whole hall and my gaze stopped at the entrance.

She was exiting and entering the doors every five minutes. I did not know what was going on and why she was doing what she was doing. I watched closely and saw some strange styles of walking and some strange facial expressions. She seemed like she was mono-acting. She exited as somebody and entered as somebody else. What on earth was she up to?

Gradually, a few more people gathered around me and we watched her from behind one of the trees. She was also muttering something to herself. She was totally oblivious of the fact that she was being watched.

Chuckles and muffled laughs were abuzz in the whole hall now. I could not stop myself any more, so I went up to her. She saw me and stopped instantly.

'Hehehehe,' she laughed, seeing me.

'Is everything all right? You were pacing in and out of the doors.'

'Oh, yes.'

'Are you sure? Were you checking the entrance? Is there anything you feel amiss? We still have time.'

'Oh, no, no, nothing.'

Totally unconvinced, I turned around and instructed the others to resume work. While I was still wondering what Tweety was up to, Mr Lamba walked up to me from behind.

'Thinking something?'

'Yes, ma'am looks a little uneasy. Is everything okay?'

'You mean the going in and out of the doorway?'

'Yes.'

'Okay. Did she have a guest list in her hand when she was doing so?'

'She had an A4 sheet ....'

'Hahahahah!' The sardarji cracked up. 'Well, she was doing what you can never imagine. You know, she's a perfectionist. She's not looking at the set-up through her eyes; she's looking at the set-up through the eyes of her brothers, sisters, uncles, aunts, friends, and the VIP guests. So, every time she walked in, she imagined somebody and what they would think when they enter.'

Holy cow! She was not a perfectionist, she was nuts!

I heard myself saying, 'But I hope I don't have to make any changes thinking what Mr Khanna or Mr Kapoor is going to like because I signed the contract with you.'

'Oh, nothing like that. I will handle her.'

We were nearing the end of the design and the light designer was now at work to give the whole room hues of amber and gold like a maple orchard. All set, all done, we were ready for the party! Leaving all to the manager of the evening, I retired for the day and made my way back home after exchanging warm goodbyes with the couple.

The next day, I got a call of thanks, telling me how amazing it was. All accounts were settled amicably and we parted to meet again closer to the wedding, which was in twenty days.

Kahani Mein Twist

A week later, I got a call from Tweety.

She was breathless and really low and not chirpy at all. She started talking slowly, totally unlike her volcanic self, 'There is bad news and good news. The bad news is that my daughter's engagement is broken,' and she started crying, 'Eve has ditched Adam as they can not get along,' and she wailed. And then, suddenly, she stopped wailing and said, 'Now here's the good news. We have found a new match for our daughter and the wedding will be exactly on the same date as planned and we have to do a re-engagement.'

I was ready to say *no* as I had not been given a chance to react, to express despair or happiness, not that she cared about that. All she wanted was to be heard. I simply could not do another design meeting with her.

'Now for the good news,' she went on and laughed hysterically. Wait a minute. Wasn't the good news that she had found a match for her daughter? I was a little confused. Tweety continued, 'We are doing the engagement two days from now at the same venue where you did the engagement last week and I want the same decor that you did for me last week. There's no need to meet. I know you will do a good job.'

So, it is the same decor, same venue, just not the same groom. Isn't life simple?

13

Battling a Hostage Situation

One day we got an enquiry from a diamond baron from Surat:

Dear,

We really like your work showcased on your website; we are enamoured by our Indian cultural heritage and want the same for my daughter's wedding as most of our guests will be from overseas. I want to recreate an Indian palace here in Surat. Land is no problem, we can give you as much area as you want. Would you be able to help me in this? For the same, I am ready to come to Delhi asap to check some samples.

Thank you.
Shekhar

Battling a Hostage Situation

I invited him over to spend a day at our office to see our craftsmanship and work. Emails were exchanged and on a mutually acceptable day, the meeting was set.

His manager coordinated everything. The baron was to stay in the royal suite of Taj Mansingh Hotel. He was visiting for three days.

Day 1

The meeting was set in the meeting room of the Taj Mansingh Hotel at 9 a.m. I was expecting a hefty fellow as he sounded gruff on the phone. The clock struck nine and in a few minutes, a tiny man with a large head and curly hair walked in. Dressed in a red-and-white chequered shirt and a pair of black trousers, he walked in quickly and sat in the head chair of the meeting table.

I said, 'Hi.'

'Hello, I'm Shekhar.'

With great difficulty, I hid my surprise and said, 'Nice to meet you.'

'Yes, same here. You must be Rasika.'

At least one of us looked how we sounded, I thought to myself. I got over my surprise quickly and started the conversation. 'So how was your flight?' and the usual pleasantries. (I knew he had flown in on a chartered plane.)

My assistant joined us and was ready to start the slideshow on the big screen with different palaces of India so that we could understand what kind of palace he liked. He went through every palace very quickly. He seemed to be more inclined towards the Rajput style. And finally settled for the Hawa Mahal.

I complimented him on his taste but explained that we would definitely have to modify it a bit as the Hawa Mahal has thousands of windows hence the name Palace of Breeze. We could prettify it by adding coloured mirrors to it and some painted tiles. Upon further discussions, we decided that we needed to sample it.

The meeting finished around 5 p.m. and we headed straight to our workshop; the carpenter and craftsman were waiting for us to start the sampling. They had the whole night to create one panel of the Hawa Mahal. The baron was supposed to meet us the next evening. I had told him clearly that some sampling would be ready and some would be prepared in front of him as there was not enough time for the prep.

In our previous meeting, while we had a sandwich and cappuccino, all the little guy had was at least ten cups of black tea till noon—no food, not even a cookie. So, I arranged fifty tea bags and two Thermoses full of hot water. We were so right in doing that.

The little guy turned up bang on time with his manager. He got down from the car and quickly walked up to the table which was set up. His big head with a curly mop was very distracting. Do short guys maintain such a hairdo to appear taller? But there are many short men who are geniuses. He pulled up a chair and sat down with folded arms, as if to watch a movie. We briefly exchanged greetings and kept standing. On seeing the sample structure of the Hawa Mahal in front of him, he exclaimed, 'It's *pink*!'

'Yes, that's the heritage colour of Jaipur, also known as the Pink City, and that's the original colour of the Hawa Mahal.'

'No, I don't want pink. I want peach.'

'That's not a problem; we can create the colour palette of your choice.'

Half of the structure was repainted to a peach-sandstone kind of shade. After many peaches got rejected, we found the perfect peach.

The baron was quite a chugging machine. He kept chugging on his cigars non-stop and sipping tea. He seemed to live on cigar and tea only. His head seemed a little bigger to me all of a sudden though I dismissed it as an illusion. I noticed the gel in his hair had dried up, so the curly mop looked untamed and the head popped out noticeably.

He called me to sit next to him and started talking about his daughter fondly. 'My daughter is a princess. I want to get a seat for her and her groom to be designed especially with real gold thread. I will get the real gold thread for you and under the supervision of my managers, the seat will be worked upon with the thread.'

It sounded so exciting. I beamed and said, 'Of course, why not? The royal princess deserves nothing less.'

By evening, the colour, the fabric, and the flowers were all decided. The chugging machine was extremely critical and inquisitive to the level of being nosy; he wanted to know the cost of the paint, etc. The questions the baron asked were not those of a client but of a manufacturer or fabricator. He wanted to know which wood, which metal, what weight, which paper, which paint, what company—everything.

I asked for a ten-day period of time for everything to be put into order. The baron bid us adieu and went back to his hotel. We did not meet him the next day but we had a lot of call coordination between him and his managers, so we gave whatever information they needed over the phone and got on with the business of the presentation. A nominal fee was agreed upon for our ten-day work and we gave it our best and prepared a fantabulous presentation with waterworks.

***

As most of the guests in attendance were to be from Abu Dhabi, utmost care had to be taken to give privacy to their women. I believe they were his buyers; otherwise, he would not invite the whole kingdom of Arabia and go to these lengths.

We were told to create two separate large dining and reception halls with a common lobby. Both sexes were to be in different halls. The men were not supposed to interact with the women and vice versa since it was prohibited.

The baron told me, 'Your DJ and entertainment team has to be all women as they will be in the women's hall and playing music for them. For the rest of the place, I want surround sound.'

The floor plans were created for 1,860 square metres of area with a common lobby with a waterfall in the front at the landing point.

Over the next ten days, we created the designs and simultaneously cost sheets were drawn up and various engineers were roped to create the pyrotechnics, waterfalls, and electric curtains.

A 150-slide presentation was made in less than ten days and a team of three was selected to make the presentation; the date was set and tickets were issued. The team went and gave a magnificent presentation. Guess what happened next?

I got a frantic call from my team saying that the baron wanted them to stay there for the next six months and offered them a proper office, a home, a mind-blowing salary, a car, and a surprise gift at the end. They would get all this if they could stay there, put a team together, and execute the wedding with the available resources in Surat.

My team was perturbed and amused, wondering if that offer was for our company or to them as individuals. I understood what had happened and I warned them, 'He wants to make you three his pets, trying the use and throw technique. Tell him to speak with me.'

I called Shekhar's secretary and asked him what the hell was going on. He said, 'Oh, he loves the presentation and wants to keep these people and get it executed.'

Executed! All I could think of was the dangling necks of my teammates. I told him, 'Listen, they are people, not roosters whom you can trap just like that. Send them back at once and we will sign the contract officially with the said amount, followed by a bank transfer of the instalment for shipping and execution. The team will come one month before the designated date to commence the work and we will take several rounds in between.'

The manager relayed this information to Shekhar who immediately came on the line and said, 'Hello, madam, I was just easing your stress. Tell them to stay on, finish my daughter's wedding, and go back.'

'No, sir, they have to return and go on an official trip with proper paperwork and drawings.'

'That all will be done here; we have the people here.'

He was being so unreasonable! After a lot of convincing, he said, 'Okay, okay, I'm keeping the presentation to show to my daughter,' and instructed his manager to issue the return tickets to my team. The manager eventually handed over a booklet of tickets to my team and said, 'Come any time you are ready, so now you can travel up and down for finalizing all the designs.'

Leaving the presentation behind was a mistake, but at that time it sounded like a barter—Presentation for Lives! I got my team back which cost me a 150-slide presentation, but at least I got people back alive. But to Surat? I do not even want to go there for free with this experience.

The baron compensated them for their hard work which they handed over to the office accounts, but later I realized why he did that. When my team returned safely, we decided to drop this project due to the hostage situation, goony behaviour, and mafia-type feeling surrounding this whole wedding. We sent a polite email withdrawing our services. I did not hear back from them either.

I was uneasy that they did not reply, hence two months before the wedding, I told my brother-in-law, 'Next month any time you are going to Surat, please check this location out. That's the location my team went for the recce but that project didn't work out.'

He used to frequently visit Surat for business purposes. So we waited. The date of the wedding was December end. Around that time, my brother-in-law went to Surat on an official trip and sent me a selfie with a set-up in the backdrop which resembled a pink palace in Rajasthan.

He sent me the image via WhatsApp with this message: 'Hey, you were right about the story, Nancy Drew! The prick has it all figured out.'

I recited a poem in my head:

He looked like a goblin right from the start,
The moment he walked in,
I knew he was a farce.
All that guy needed was the design
And the know-how.
After all, he was a diamantaire,
He knew a good design
When he saw one.

14

Fault in the Stars?

It was the perfect setting for a meeting at the Imperial Hotel in New Delhi. The meeting was to be held together with families of the bride and groom. We reached early and took a big table at the coffee shop to accommodate around fifteen people. Then we set up a beautiful floral arrangement in the centre of the table. It was about 4 feet long and had transparent glass props to give it some character as it was also a showcase, a mock set-up of our work. Like a picture can speak a thousand words, one great arrangement gives the client a taste of our style.

The parties arrived five minutes apart with the bride and groom. We started the meeting as always with a short presentation with my teammates furiously making notes of every whim and fancy thrown our way. I found it odd that the father of the bride was the only person who did not speak. He must be the quiet type.

All was pretty much decided and everyone stepped out to the lawns where the functions would be held. The father lagged behind. He was a big, chubby man. I fell back and started walking with him as I was inquisitive. 'So, Mr Khanna, what did you like and did not like about our presentation? Give me an idea as your opinion also matters.'

'Well, my dear, I can tell you what I don't like certainly; about what I like, it really doesn't matter.'

I was very curious now. 'Yes, do tell me what you don't like. We will make sure not to include it.'

'Are you sure you can do that?'

'Of course, I'm the wedding planner! I can plan the wedding to everybody's liking.'

'The groom, I don't like the groom.'

I was dumbstruck.

'Sir, Mr Khanna, what are you saying?'

He stopped and turned to face me.

'Yes, I don't want this marriage. Can you tell me how I can stop it?'

'But why? All seem happy, your daughter seems happy.'

'No, you don't know. He is a Casanova, he has dated every girl in this city ...'

I interrupted him, 'Mr Khanna, all boys are like that till they meet *the one*.'

'No, you have no idea. Anyway, go on. Get along with your business and we never spoke about anything, okay?'

Utterly horrified and confused, I hurried towards the lawn where everybody was waiting for me.

'Sorry, I got a call,' and we continued with the nitty-gritty of the planning.

On the way back in the car, I told my team, 'Guess what, guys, this wedding may not happen. Did you find the boy weird?'

Kanchan sprang up and said, 'No, not at all. He was so cute.'

I looked at her with a sly smile. 'Aha, how cute?'

She blushed and dived into her notes.

Another one asked me, 'Why, ma'am? Why won't this wedding happen? They have called us tomorrow for the financial meeting.'

'Nothing, just a hunch.'

Maybe the father was very possessive about her and considered nobody would ever be good enough for his daughter. He was sulking like a little boy.

All was going according to plan, the functions were scheduled to start soon, even the advances were paid by the father himself. But I had a hunch that he was up to something. *What's he going to do?* I kept wondering. How could I save this marriage from a possessive father?

The wedding invitation cards were being sent out as the event was in a few weeks. Though I was apprehensive about the explosion he was planning, I kept quiet because my team would have told me not to go for it. So, with the secret locked in my heart, we went ahead.

On the day of the *shagun*, the father looked excited for the first time. I felt glad that he had finally accepted the groom, so I congratulated him. I said, 'Finally! Your big responsibility is over.'

He laughed out loud. 'Yes, yes, it's over!'

This was the second time we spoke as I had been steering clear of him. He patted my shoulder and put his finger on his lips and walked away. Later, he said, 'Time will tell, time will tell. Have you told anybody? Anyone, your team, your husband?'

'No, of course not. I knew you were joking with me.'

'Okay, good, keep it like that. I will in no way let my daughter go home with this idiot!'

Idiot? Oh my god! He was far from being happy. Was he going to get him kidnapped or what? I eagerly went to the door when I heard the sound of *dhols*, which marked the entry of the *baraat*. I decided to keep an eye on the poor chap.

The groom was respectfully brought to the stage where he sat and his shagun ceremony started. The panditji asked, 'Ji, what's your date of birth?'

When that was revealed, he took the groom's mother aside. God knows what he said to her because she frantically called her husband and other relatives and they got into a huddle for forty-five minutes. Surprisingly the bride's father was smiling throughout. I was sure that the pandit was planted by him to make some damaging revelations about the marriage. And it seemed to work because the groom's mother seemed very superstitious. Because all I could hear was, 'Oho, now what do we do', and other concerns in the same vein.

Wow! Well played, Mr Khanna! Let us see who wins.

Suddenly, the groom got up and stormed out of the hall. Oh shit, it was over! All were watching in disbelief and finally, I heard the sound of the dhol again while I kept telling myself: What a family drama!

The groom walked in dancing with his bride and they both held each other's hand tightly and sat on the mattresses on the stage. The groom told the pandit, 'Do our pooja together,' and with folded hands said, 'Dear Panditji, I don't give a shit about your prediction. Just do as I say.'

I turned my head to the right and looked straight at Mr Khanna and smiled at him very disapprovingly. He was neither chuckling nor smiling; he just looked defeated. I casually walked up to Mr Khanna and told him, 'Keep the faith.'

I do not know what the pandit said, but kudos to the groom. He did what his heart said. Such a dreamboat couple.

15

How Mother Gothel Got Me Tangled

This incident was one of the turning points in my life as it made me wiser. I was doing the wedding of a powerful politician's daughter—the daughter of his girlfriend actually. I was called for a meeting by an MP, a friend of the bride's mother, and a good client of mine, an elegant and smart lady. She requested me to do a splendid job as the wedding was one of the most high-profile ones with a guest list including the prime minister and other bigwigs.

We were excited for the project. We were doing well by the grace of God. And it had been only a couple of years since we had started our company in 2005. We prepared the presentations, hand sketches, and fabrics for the presentation. At that time, the presentation mode was so real that you could smell the paint on the sketches the artist had drawn for a set-up. Sometimes we used to dry wet sketches in the air conditioning of the car.

Finally, on the day of the meeting, things went very smoothly. We met the beautiful mother and the daughter, and we were absolutely delighted to be a part of the affair. The wedding also went smoothly. We got a warm thank you and a goodbye as gracious as the lady herself, but little did we know that she was an enchantress like Mother Gothel from the movie *Tangled*.

A few days passed and there was no call or communication with them, so I called the MP. She said, 'Hi, so nice to hear from you. Oh, your bill. I'll just ask her and get back to you, my dear. They were awfully busy with the wedding and the guests leaving, don't worry.'

So, I waited for her call.

She called me the next day. 'Hey, what are you doing? Come over if you are around.'

She lived in a posh south Delhi locality so I dropped by after a long day of hard work. My office was strategically located in Vasant Kunj, so distances were not really a problem. She was extremely polite and an avid collector of art. Her home spoke of style and good taste. I crossed the gallery of cars, the manicured lawn, the beautiful bougainvillea walkway in the driveway, and reached her door and rang the bell. She opened the door herself and took me by my arm straight into her living room. She was tall, fit, and had a genuine smile.

After refreshments were served, she came straight to the point and all of a sudden, her bright, chirpy face became sad and serious.

She said, 'I have called you here to protect you,' while twisting the rings on her fingers.

'Protect me?'

'Yes, I'm really sorry, it's all my fault. I should have never put you on to those people. I never thought that they would do this to you, especially as I am involved.'

Then she went on to say, 'So tell me, what is the most important thing in your life?'

'Many things—my family, my business, my freedom, most of all. Actually, all are important.'

'What if all of this is taken away from you? How would you feel?'

I turned numb. Suddenly, I felt like I had fallen from the sky and landed with a thud on her manicured lawn, on my bum.

'Look, dear, they are dangerous people. When I called them for the bill, they said, "What money? Nobody asks for money from us. Doesn't she know whom she is dealing with?" You know, Rasika, I told them I get all my parties done from you and that you are such a genuine girl. How can you guys deceive her like this?

'So, my friend said, "Tell her to forget about it and that it is something she should completely forget to dream about also."'

I was almost in tears but I said nothing at that time. I could not utter a word. The lady kept explaining but I had blanked out. These guys run the nation! What country do I live in?

I somehow managed to end the meeting and left. I drove down straight to the client's house. (Young blood in rage!) I rang the bell and gave my card to the guard, who went in, returned, and said, 'They are saying they are not at home.'

'Ask them when they will be home so I can come back then.'

The guard returned and said, 'They are saying they will never be home.' He quietly added, 'Madam, they will never be home for you. Aren't you the one who did all the wedding planning for them? I wish I could have stopped you.'

I figured out that I was stuck but I followed up for a few days as I just could not let go of my hard-earned money, till I got The Call.

It was the MP. 'Hi, darling. I have heard you have been doing rounds of the house for your payment?'

'Yes, definitely. I did not want to involve you as it's not your fault.'

'Oh, no, no! These are very dangerous people. If you ask for money, you will die.'

I thought, *Yes, you are telling me when the damage is done?*

'I got a call from "the boyfriend", who is also a very famous politician. He was asking for the name of your company and address. I said I don't know. I never asked her that.

'When I didn't give him the name of your company and address, he said, "I'll find it if I have to and, by the way, tell her not to come near my house or ever call. Otherwise, from tomorrow, nobody will know that a company by the name of @#$% and a girl by the name of @#$ existed." He means it. You will get enough opportunities in life, you have just started. Let it go!'

I was so taken aback that I could not react. She hung up and I kept staring into space. I could not do anything. Could I hire a lawyer to fight that minister at that level? I just gave up and put it behind me.

16

Pressing the Wrong Button

How does a lady full of poise and grace turn into a hell cat? I will get straight to D-day, everything else before that was a cakewalk. What I did not know was that a person so graceful could have such a wicked side to them.

I was just two years into my career and keen to prove my worth to the world. I would give my best to every task laid out in front of me. I fulfilled my commitments to the T. This particular set-up was very interesting. We had to make a large button in the centre of the hall's ceiling. It was a nearly 2-metre-wide metal button stuffed with foam and cotton to make it cushiony and then wrapped in golden satin. It looked beautiful with Christmas lights pulled across the whole hall, engulfing the entire place in streams of lights. The button was the hero of the party and we were delighted with the profound effect it created in its subtleness. The lights were pulled equidistantly from one another, forming a large overhead marquee of lights under which the grand reception was to take place.

One event manager friend of mine, Priya, who has a company in Singapore, came to visit me in the evening towards completion and commented that it was by far one of the most exquisite settings she had seen. The centrepieces were round like a button again, with white hydrangeas on every table with round ball candles all around. I had been up all night with my team to make sure the execution was flawless.

At the same time, the hostess of the party came to the venue to have a look at the settings. I was happy with the outcome and went straight up to her and welcomed her.

She was wearing a traditional Indian suit in olive green with a pair of large round glasses resting on the bridge of her fine nose. She had a mop of short and crisp white, curly hair on her head, which looked slightly small on her body that day. Maybe because she was tall and well-built and the suit she wore was flowing, she looked less elegant than I had seen her before.

I said, 'You are so early. It's only five and the reception is not till seven.'

'I wanted to check everything.'

'You are more than welcome as we are nearly finished. Just a few tucks and loose ends are left, which will be done in an hour at the most.'

She looked at me and then went right to the middle of the hall and looked up at the button. 'You call this a button?'

I was taken aback by the rude question and replied, 'Yes.'

She asked, this time in a slightly raised voice, 'You call this a button, Rasika?'

'Yes, Mrs Iyenger, it is a button, same size and dimensions and same colour as we discussed. Doesn't it look so to you?'

She said no and pounced on me, and what happened next was earth-shattering.

She screamed, 'You call this a button? You call this a button? You crazy girl, this is not a button!' She came charging at me like a barbarian and stabbed me with her ballpoint pen's nib on my upper arm.

I bent over in pain and put a hand on my arm where she struck me. I was wearing a sleeveless shirt, so it was easy for the nib to pierce my skin. I looked at her, stunned. I removed my hand and a trickle of blood went down my arm and fell on the carpet. How could a small nib make such an impact?

Tears rolled down my eyes and then I could hear her voice again. Oh, now she was going to cry! She was going to pretend as if I had killed her. I kept staring at her and was at a loss for words. I looked around and saw everyone had frozen around me—the waiters, my workers, and my assistant standing with her hand covering her mouth.

That lady kept babbling, going ballistic over nothing. I got over the humiliation and took a few steps towards her and stood directly in front of her with my hand still clasped on my arm.

'You don't think this is a button?' I asked her sternly yet softly. 'Are you sure? I will give you a few seconds to evaluate if this is a button or not. Look up, Mrs Iyenger. Is this a button or not?' My teeth were clenched and I was not even blinking.

'No, you crazy girl, this is not a button.'

'Pack up!' I screamed at the top of my voice. I clapped my bloodied hands together and said, 'Pack up, guys, I mean it. Please move it, move it!'

Pressing the Wrong Button

Kanchan came running to me and said, 'You mean pack up? Meaning we leave?'

'Pack up meaning *bring the set-up down!*'

Kanchan shuddered and said, 'Got it!' But gave me a look like I had flipped.

I ignored that and said, '*Move!*'

She ran and started yelling instructions to the team, '*Seedi lao, upar chado, jaldi karo, sab kuch utaro!*' (Get the ladder, climb up, hurry up, and take off everything!)

When Mrs Iyenger heard the instructions, she came flying at me. This time, I was ready to punch her if she laid a finger on me. 'You mad, crazy girl! How dare you? What do you think of yourself? So what if I lost my cool? By chance I had a pen in my hand and it struck you. Don't pretend that you are going to die!'

'I am not the one who is dying here, Mrs Iyenger. Goodbye.'

And I turned around and walked out of the hall. Priya followed me closely behind and said, 'Oh my god! This doesn't happen in Singapore! Are you sure? They are tearing down the set-up. She won't allow it.'

As we kept walking out towards the escalators, hurried steps came behind me. It was the hotel staff. 'Madam, please, their party is about to start ...'

'I am sorry, I cannot help you. All I can assure you is that in one hour you will get a neat and clean hall like nothing ever happened there. And yes, you can remove my blood from your carpet because I didn't ask my team to remove that.'

The whole hall was cleansed of any sign of decor within an hour. The guests arrived, the party went on, and there were murmurs throughout about how stingy Mrs Iyenger was that she did not even put a pot of flowers to welcome the new couple, who were equally taken aback. There was no stage, no centrepiece, no lights, no flowers and, of course, no button.

17

To the Rescue, à la Sholay Style

When they came to meet us at our office, I saw a very smartly dressed boy with a friend of ours who introduced us to the groom-to-be, Noel. Though he was French, he was more desi than any desi boy. He wanted a proper Indian wedding with a paanwala and fireworks.

He seemed happy but I could see a deep undertone of melancholy in his eyes. He seemed a little different. During the meeting, he stepped out and I could see from my office window that he was trying to light up a cigarette. (Our office building is tucked in a corner of the farm and is built like a hut with a man-made waterbody surrounding it with golden fish. A small bridge over the pond leads to the office door.)

The farm has my dogs—Virtue, the Labrador, and Mighty, the Great Dane. Nandu Chacha takes care of them and my husband's mare, SOL—Spirit of Love. There is enough recreation to always keep us happy. All thanks to Yash and his love for animals.

Coming back to Noel, he was wandering around, looking at the various props lying around, and ended up playing with Vuccy (Virtue) and Mighty.

I told my friend to chill and we stepped out with our coffee mugs and waited for Noel to decompress.

He walked towards us with great energy and said, 'Okay, guys, let's get on with our work!' Before I handed him his coffee, I asked him if he would like to wash his hands and dust his clothes, as the dogs had actually been all over him though he loved it. He agreed. We returned inside and started taking our positions around the table.

Noel joined us after freshening up and the next two hours followed with an arduous meeting to finalize the plans: the bachelor's party (in which I gave Yash the lead so they could organize their boy stuff), the mehndi, the sangeet cocktail, and the wedding.

I was not involved in the bachelor's gig which, according to Yash was too wild. The mehndi was a couple of days later, so everyone got forty-eight hours to sober up after the bachelor's.

On the mehndi ceremony day, the groom was getting smothered by the yellow *vattana* (gram flour paste), looking totally dazed and stoned. I figured he was hungover and so was everyone out there. Lots of music, beers, and hundreds of cocktails later, the mehndi came to an end with Noel lying flat on one of the divan seats, not moving.

His parents were too drunk to look after him, and so were his friends. When I expressed my concerns to Yash and Kanchan, they said, 'Stay out of it!'

'But what if he needs an ambulance?'

They said, 'It's their business. You are not his mother and probably they all always end up like this, so no need for you to fret. Let's go to the back lawn and see what's going on at the cocktail site.' I reluctantly started walking with Kanchan, staying worried about Noel. Thankfully, I overheard Yash asking my manager Dharmender to check on the groom.

On *sangeet*, the next day, Noel looked all fresh like nothing had happened. With a great sigh of relief, I left the cocktail party to this fun-loving lot and headed back home as the next day was D-day.

On the day of the wedding, the *sehra-bandi* was scheduled at 6 p.m. and the *baraat* was to leave for the wedding venue by 8 p.m.

We were at the wedding venue, which was an hour away from Noel's home. I got a call from Dharmender, 'Madam, can you and sir come here?'

'Dharmender, have you gone mad? The baraat will be here in a couple of hours. How can I leave the site? And why do you want me there?'

'Madam, both of you should please get here. The groom is drunk out of his mind!'

'That's his problem and his family's, not ours. Just find someone there and inform them about Noel's condition.'

Meanwhile, Yash got a call on his mobile phone from the mutual friend, 'Brother, please come, he is going to die!'

What? *Die?*

We left the site to my reliable team and made a dash for the groom's house.

We hurriedly climbed up the stairs to his room, which was beautifully made up like a studio apartment on the terrace with a garden with real grass and a small outdoor jacuzzi. It was like a Chinese villa. The garden was where the sehra-bandi set-up had been put, and to our utter shock, nobody was there. From a distance, I could see someone's back on the parapet. A tall figure ran towards us. It was Dharmender. 'Madam! Sir! Over there, hurry! Sir is sitting over there.'

I ran towards the parapet and from either side, we put our hands on Noel's shoulders. He was sitting on the parapet with his legs dangling, almost ready to jump.

'Noel! What are you thinking?'

'I'm looking at the sky, the stars are coming out, the sun is setting …'

And I cut in, 'Yes and you are late for your wedding!' Meanwhile, Dharmender and Yash held a solid grip on him so that he could not jump.

'Hah, let those fuckers wait.'

He reeked of alcohol and he had a bottle of wine in his hand, and a few bottles were strewn around. Gosh, he had had wine like beer! He was quite sloshed. How do we sober him up? His friend was sitting on the floor of the terrace with his head in his hands.

I asked Dharmender, 'Wasn't it Dharmendra who wanted to commit suicide in that movie?'

Yash glared at me

Noel said, 'I don't think I should go ahead with it. I don't think I should. Just call her and tell her that I am dead or something!'

Apparently, some friends who had already been informed of Noel's position were holding the fort downstairs, preventing anybody from coming up. With great effort, Noel put one leg inside, like he was sitting astride a horse and started pretending that he was on one. He did not know any better because of his state.

To the Rescue, à la Sholay Style   133

The boys finally managed to get him down and got his sherwani straightened and buttoned up, which he had flung over himself shabbily. He had this amazing quality to not reveal he was out of his wits. He went through the *havan* and pooja and then he was loaded into the car and carried to the wedding venue where he went into a deep sleep.

At the venue, it was a task to get him up and then upon the horse. By now, people were a little suspicious. Once on the horse, he did not want to get down; once down from the horse, he did not want to walk to the *mandap*. The bride walked in and the *jaimala* happened somehow with a shaky groom. I wondered if love really is blind, but then she might have been hoping to change him once she was with him.

Later, when the *pheras* took place, the groom was mentally just not there. That day, other than managing the event, I was doing everything else—managing the groom, managing the poor bride, assuring the family all will be well, and being a friend and a well-wisher.

The brave bride and I exchanged a lot of looks and I gave her a reassuring thumbs up every time because somewhere inside, I felt she had faith. And what if he did need a reason to live? And the reason could be her.

Only after sending off the *doli* could we reach back home. Next day, we received a call from our friend and he said that Noel had just woken up and it was around 4 p.m. He had missed the lunch which was organized by the family to introduce the bride. 'He is, however, thanking you guys for helping him take the right plunge and saving him from the wrong one.'

Yash was on the call. All he said was, 'As long as he stays away from suicidal thoughts, bro. Now he needs to be responsible for Kajal's sake.'

We were happy to help, but the experience haunted us for a long time. We had never saved a man from killing himself before.

18

Mrs Voldemort

Posh people are not so posh from the inside. I still wake up sometimes with her voice, more like a hyena's call, ringing in my ears. And many a time, I look up to the heavens and ask God why he led me to her. Sometimes you realize much later that all things happen for a reason, but with this woman, I am still left wondering. With her I went against my gut feeling. I thought: *Let us see what she has got. She cannot really screw me that badly.* All I can say today is that I was horribly wrong. I saw the signs but had my blinkers on. I got overwhelmed by the kind of money I was about to earn and the challenge. But I simply did not bargain for the wicked, rich witch.

It was December 2009 when the wedding was scheduled. It was a Sikh wedding. I realized during the first meeting that this project was going to be a tough one, but we took up the challenge nevertheless.

The challenge being that the wedding was slated for 1 January 2010, which meant directly after new-year parties. The bride's mother was a posh Sikh lady and quite a fierce one.

She had said, 'Don't you dare get a new-year hangover and ruin my daughter's wedding. The reason I'm trusting you is that you seem the responsible type.'

Well, we thought we could handle the event but we did not know what we were in for. We had the trucks run out to the venue on time a day before the event despite the freezing cold. The work started well on time on the morning of 31 December. We were there for the groundwork to get it started. I made sure all placements were done and then the craftsmen took over and started the work according to the site details.

I left in the evening to unwind and prepare for my New Year's Eve party with my friends. We had planned the night at a friend's place for bonfire, barbeque, and drinks, with plenty of good music. We had a great time and we decided not to sleep as I had to reach the site by 6 a.m. for the 9 a.m. finish.

By 3–3.30 a.m., we felt sluggish and thought it that it might do us some good if we slept for a couple of hours as our home was close by. So, we went back home. I was woken up by a phone call at 5 a.m. and a shrill screech on the other side of the line.

'How dare you! How dare you go to a party? Now you must be drunk. You will be hungover and now you will not be able to finish my set-up,' and she went on and on and on.

I was totally fine and ready to be on site in an hour. But how to tell her that? She was just too uncouth, so to hell with her. I was not giving any explanation!

She went on to say, 'I'm standing here at the site. There is nobody here, nobody is working. Are all your guys dead? If they are not, I will shoot them!'

Shit, I should not have taken a 1 January site. What if her pumpkin was hungover and drunk? Meanwhile, I knew it was all bullshit that my guys were not there.

I scrambled up, quickly brushed my teeth, changed my clothes, and wore some layers to beat the cold. I woke my husband up on my way out and asked him to come to the site in a bit. 'I need you. It's a *Godzilla*!'

I reached the site and there was no sign of any disturbance. There were guys at the entrance putting flowers, the tents were up, the flower guys were doing the drape edgings with flowers, and all the tables and chairs were set. Though it was very foggy, the work was going on; the linen was not put yet as it would have become wet. Everything was in proper order!

Then suddenly out of the fog, a hooded figure in black track pants and a Black jacket walked up to me and lifted her head. It was *she*! I could feel my soul screaming. But I could not flee, I could not scream, I could not cry. I could only smile reassuringly and manage a 'Good Morning'.

The figure croaked, 'You better finish this or else …'

I just walked away and stood with my craftsman who was up on a ladder and told him that he was doing a great job.

He said, 'Madam, it's so cold. See my hands, they are blue. I'm not able to move my fingers to cut the stems of the flowers.'

I told him to stop and rub his hands together and go by the small fire they had lit on the side to keep themselves warm.

He said, 'I did it once. She saw me and screamed at me. *Na baba na, mere ko maar degi.*' (No, no, she will kill me.)

I told him to go slyly. Out of nowhere, she appeared and rattled and shook the ladder on which he was standing and said, 'Are you trying to ruin my set-up?'

I said, 'Please, Mrs Bhalla, everything is on track. Why are you panicking?'

She lashed out at me and before I could respond, a phone rang somewhere above me. It was one of my craftsmen's who was on a ladder. He answered the phone and said, 'Hello, yes. I'm at the site. I'll talk to you later.' That was all he said.

The witch saw it and, to my horror, attacked him. She pushed the ladder so hard that the guy almost stumbled down but fortunately could balance himself. However, his phone fell out of his hand and fell straight into a bucket of cold water under the ladder. I was thankful the ladder did not fall on me and that my craftsman did not get hurt. By now, I was sure she was mentally unstable.

After some time, far ahead down the food area, I heard screams again. I ran there, and to my astonishment found all arrangements on the food counters had toppled over and Mrs Voldemort was pulling flowers out of them and throwing them here and there and swearing. I asked her, 'What's wrong? Why are you destroying these arrangements!'

'I want them low not high!'

I told her they would not be visible if they were low, and she said, 'It's my party. I want it low.'

'It's not my or my *karigars*' fault. We have made it according to our discussions, but we never said we won't make it low. By doing what you are doing, you have killed the flowers and I cannot reuse them even to create low arrangements.'

Miraculously, she stopped, swore once more, and walked away.

My Agenda: Complete and Leave

The sun was coming out and the flowers looked cheerful and happy, but my karigars were frightful and sad. We were near completion, but Mrs Voldemort was nowhere to be seen.

Whom do I hand over the site to as we are all set? I wondered. I decided to call Mr Bhalla and informed him that all was done and my manager had the *varmala*s needed for the couple. He thanked me.

I just did not want to speak to her or even see her after what she had done here. I finished my job as per my contract, left the venue, and headed straight to my bed, my blanket, my room, and blissful sleep finally.

A few days later, Mr Bhalla called me to meet him at his home to settle my accounts. To my horror, when I walked in I was taken straight to his room! When I entered his bedroom, it looked more like a hospice. Mr Bhalla was in bed with broken arms in loops, completely plastered from the shoulders. Mrs Voldemort looked mellow but was frying me with her eyes. He told his wife to take out a chequebook.

'Cut her cheque,' he ordered.

Then she obeyed like a well-trained cat. Tore the end and handed it over to me. Correct amount to my shock.

I asked him what happened, how, and when?

I just wished him a speedy recovery and showed myself out, wondering if he too was on some ladder and she pushed him.

I focused on my steps as I was taking the flight down lest I fall too. I headed straight to my car and finally found my breath back!

19

Tenali Rama Caught Red-handed

This chapter is about a very grand hotel situated in the heart of Delhi and run by the most horrible person ever born on the face of this earth—Amit Mehra.

Back in 2005–06, when I was starting out, I had big dreams and aspirations. Life has treated me well. I am happy with the little sunshine that God has given me, making my dream of becoming a wedding planner come true. It was then that I came across this monster. I had a sound team of amazing florists and artisans. Their talent gave me all the confidence. All the commitments made to people by us as a team were because of their support and skills. One day a meeting was set up with this clown, with thin and meek black glasses over his Tenali Rama face and jet black hair combed down, which stuck to his skull as if they were drenched in oil. I sat in his small office with the paperwork and presentations and the contract, when he opened his mouth and croaked: 'How can you handle this hotel? Do you know what your competition is here? Do you know the class and quality of this hotel?'

'Yes, I do, that's why I am here. Our work is seven-star and that's why I am sitting here in your five-star hotel.'

I had given him a five-star rating and myself seven-stars. Hahaha, what the heck! I am telling the truth and I choose my venues of work, and that is what I said to him.

'You know, we have this Molly—Polly—on the panel. She does amazing work and she gives me 25 per cent of everything she earns. Hotel commission is separate, mind you. Can you afford to do that?'

'I can try. Let's see how it goes. So, shall we form a final contract if it's okay with you? I have the stamp and all necessary documentation.'

'Fine, but I don't see you getting successful here. You've just started out, no experience, no confidence. It doesn't seem like you'll last in this business.'

I had a direct link to get on the panel through a client who was friends with the hotel owner, but I chose to take the other way, through hard work and perseverance. I remember my grandma had told me once: 'People will say things to you to make you feel bad and they will try to break you, nobody will praise you. If you have a heart strong enough to hear all that, then only should you start your work, beta.'

Holy cow! Bingo! This is exactly what my grandma had warned me about, so a smile erupted on my face and I said, 'Don't worry so much about how my company will fare here. You might have to worry about how the other vendors will stay once we start working here.'

I reassured him about his percentage and his hotel's percentage separately and the deal was signed. We had another hotel in our booty. Thank you, dadi ma, I love you!

Our office geared up for client meetings with the hotel. The struggle and the fight started over the meetings vis-à-vis other panellists. The clients drove us crazy. They told us obnoxious, unreal costs which they were getting from other vendors, which was totally untrue. It was their strategy to squeeze a good deal out of you.

This is how it went: We did not do very well in the hotel, we did not get much business, and every second party was being done by Holly-Molly, the other panellist. I was in a tizzy. How could the prediction of the rat come true? I could see him laughing like a demon: 'Hahaha, I told you so!'

I was not going to take that lying down. My team was better, the presentations, workmanship, creativity—everything was way better. Then *why*? I was getting increasingly frustrated and that slimy snake called me to say, 'It seems you have not been able to get any business from here after all!'

'It takes time to break into the system, sir. The whole team is new to your hotel and we are getting there.'

He would laugh and hang up. I would go and give a pep talk to my team every time this happened. I had to get to the bottom of this. It seemed as if somebody was making sure that we did not get any work from here. We had business coming in from all places except here.

One day Yash came back from the gym and said to me, 'I have some explosive news for you. Guess who has joined my gym? Your favourite, Amit Mehra!'

I jumped on my seat and said, 'What? Good! Throw a dumbbell at him! Burn him in the sauna, bloody French-fry there. He has made my life hell!'

'After I tell you this thing, I don't need to do anything. You can make his life hell now without me laying a finger on him.'

'*How?*'

'Well, it is that he has joined the gym with his girlfriend and they work out together and the gym is their meeting ground. She is the one who is on the panel with you at that hotel. And that's why my darling wife is not getting any business from there.'

Oh shit! So all that showing me down and casting our work as bad and asking for so much money was because the slime was having an affair that too, an extramarital one. I decided then I would teach him a lesson. I would tell his wife and that would be my revenge. I was so happy that now it was his turn to run scared.

Yash said nothing. He just stared at me and let me rant. After a while, I said, 'You know what? This we can't fight as there will never be fair business here. I'm happy that I know the truth about why we are struggling so much with this particular deal, so I will just step down and let it be.'

He nodded in approval. But God had other plans. Along came a wedding reception to be held on the eve of Christmas at the hotel, where the presentation of the beloved girlfriend was disliked. It was not until I met Mrs Luthra that I realized she simply did not like Molly the panellist; she could not stand her. After sticking it out for a whole year, finally it happened.

'My god, such tacky taste, such tacky pictures. All I asked her was for a posy and she did not know what a posy is!' Mrs Luthra had a lovely British accent and she was a sheer beauty inside out, highly sophisticated, and everything for her was tacky—tacky this, tacky that—but I knew this was my chance to crack through this jinx of living with the Molly factor. I got on with the plans for the reception and made sure they were as stylish as they could get.

We created a French Riviera with bridges and cascading falls of flowers, and balconies with European windows and whatnot. Mrs Luthra was totally floored and that evening we made a mark with a set-up the hotel had not witnessed before and it gave us so much mileage.

Once the word went around, thanks to Mrs Luthra, that French theme was booked over and over with different colours. There we were, set like a cake at that hotel, and nobody could ever laugh at us any more.

It was truly a Christmas miracle for me, the way things turned around—that too in just one evening.

20

Guns and Roses

In this chapter, I will relive the memories of a wedding in Varanasi.

My team was already there along with Yash for the last one week and I was scheduled on a flight to Varanasi once the basic structuring was complete. I was received at the small airport by the client's son. We knew each other from an earlier meeting but he had been a silent presence in front of his overbearing father. It was his sister's wedding and was being hosted on the lawns of their home. As I walked out of the airport in my long black overcoat, one chilly morning, I realized how underdeveloped the smaller cities were, including the famous ones. Varanasi seemed like a different world.

I carried a small bag for myself and a suitcase full of cherries for the pudding—the expensive table decors and a few crystal pieces and velvet embroidered throws. The son graciously helped me with my luggage and we made our way to their home.

Their home was a huge building with several floors. I saw lots of clothes hanging out to dry, so I figured this was a huge family. It seemed more like a hotel, and as I walked in I saw some men in kurta pyjamas with long rifles hanging from their shoulders. It instantly reminded me of comics with dacoit stories that I used to read as a child and also of Gabbar Singh from *Sholay*.

I was a little taken aback as I did not expect my host to be someone who would have security guarding the premises of his home. I saw the huge glittering stage in the far distance. It was supposed to be around 30 metres long and in split levels, making place for the groom's family to sit on one side and the bride's family on the other, and the centre was reserved for the couple and the *jaimala* ceremony.

The wedding was next day. I found Yash, Kanchan, and Vasudha engrossed in their work at the stage area. My team had been working tirelessly for quite some time then, so I told them to take a break and we sat at the round table and was served chai and small packets of Parle-G biscuits. The chai was delicious and I was ecstatic seeing the result of my team's hard work and congratulated them.

The evening came very quickly but the caterer had not reached; he was supposed to be there by four and it was seven. Since he was coming from Delhi, we thought he must be caught in traffic. After numerous calls to the infamously famous caterer whom we always hated working with, we came to know that he and his team would reach by midnight.

This caterer had made many people cry. He was an unreliable character, so I could not for the life of me figure out why he was hired by my client. Maybe he thought, the caterer would not dare to mess with him.

So be it. Strangely, the client neither met us nor talked to us about the caterer. An army of gunmen was just walking around and we were giggling seeing how important our asses were to them. Our work was going according to the schedule.

When there was no sign of the caterer till daybreak, I got my first call from Mr Jaisingh, the client, asking if I knew anything. I informed him that he was to reach by midnight, but now he was not contactable. We had everything set, we even started setting up the food counters for the tardy fellow so that he did not have to do anything. We were hours away from the wedding and there was no sign of him.

We even got the caterer's kitchen tent ready. But where was the caterer?

Mr Jaisingh was now in the lawn. He seemed composed, in a white kurta-pyjama with a black woollen waistcoat. The ceremonies had started and there was no food! The *haldi* ceremony got over, but there was still no food. His men had arranged for bottled water and apart from that, Mr Jaisingh gave clear instructions that nothing would be served until he said otherwise.

We had a bad feeling about this. Suddenly, the caterer's trucks started rolling in at 4 p.m., two hours before the wedding to which 2,000 guests were invited. The guests already attending were anyway hungry since morning, but thankfully they were family members, so they were managing from the house kitchens.

An army of gunmen went and surrounded the trucks. On seeing them, the caterer's managers, cooks, helpers started jumping from the trucks. Those who were still inside were caught by the collar and dragged down from the truck by

the gunmen. Abuses were hurled, they were kicked and hit by the stubs of the guns, and all were now writhing in pain on the floor.

Enter Mr Jaisingh. He took out a revolver from his jacket and put it behind the ear of the manager and said, 'Where is Adit?' Adit was the caterer.

Wow ... I was transported to a Bollywood set!

The manager was fumbling and shivering and I quickly asked my men to disperse and not be anywhere around this tamasha unfolding before us. I was sure this whole thing was going to spiral out of control now. The manager had no answers. The audacity of Adit not to turn up after being twenty bloody hours late for the set-up!

Mr Jaisingh said, 'Just call him to be here by the next flight and you have two hours to live or else only your dead bodies will go back in your truck.'

Why and how did I end up with these kind of guys?

The caterer's men started to scramble to their feet and under the supervision of the gunmen they started unpacking the dishes, the tandoors, and all their other stuff.

Mr Jaisingh stayed composed and fired in the air and said, 'I'm not joking.' All hell broke loose! We were watching a spectacle à la *Sholay*.

Soon hundreds of men jumped out of the trucks and each one was running with something in his hands. They gave it all they could and the first snack rolled out at 10 p.m. though the guests had started arriving three hours ago. Meanwhile, the add-on catering service was trying to fill in with samosas and mithai, which many left untouched.

After some snooping around, we got to know that Mr Jaisingh was from a royal family. People were respectful to him as he helped the poor a lot, he was like their god. He was large-hearted but did not tolerate any nonsense.

At 10 p.m., he called Yash and me inside his home. He was sitting behind a large table and asked us the account. We gave him the account and he promptly settled it and said, 'Let me know when Adit reaches.'

I informed him, 'I think he has just reached.'

He checked if his gun was there in the pocket and got up.

He looked at me. 'You can now leave. Please also take your team with you. Just leave your manager, that boy, here.'

I told him, 'But our work is not finished! I can't leave!'

He said, 'It's finished. I am happy.'

We got up and left more like fled. I collected my team members and told my manager Dharmender—'*In kutton ko jab peetenge toh phone kar ke batana.*' (Call me when these dogs get a beating.)

He smiled and said, 'Madam, I'll send you a video.'

'Stay away from the firing and shooting, you fool, and do your work. If you get shot then what will I tell your Basanti?'

Dharmender asked, 'Why are you leaving me here to die then?'

'Mr Jaisingh knows your name and we are safe, don't worry. He is delighted with our work. Please leave after proper pack-up.'

He was thrilled that Mr Jaisingh was happy. They had given us tickets for the next morning's flight back. We were staying at the hotel he owned. After packing up, we called Dharmender from the taxi.

'You alive?'

We all laughed.

He said, 'Yes, ma'am, but I can't describe how Jaisingh has reduced Adit to a pulp. From 10 p.m. when you guys left till 2 a.m. when the *pheras* started, he beat him black and blue.'

Mr Jaisingh gave Adit a lesson for life and he paid a heavy price for it, morally and financially. I made sure to tell all my clients not to hire this bugger. That fellow got one hit for every client he had fooled and all thanks to Mr Jaisingh. And soon, Adit disappeared from the map of caterers in India.

This chapter is dedicated to all victims of Adit.

21

'Darr Ke Aage Jeet Hai'

I cannot complete this book without writing about a not-so-rare breed whose middle name is greed. My fellow event managers, beware! I did not plan to write about this but I realized it may help others who might get lured and swayed by big companies in the hope of getting business, but what really happens is that they become just a napkin for the company—use and throw. Do not ever let this happen to you.

I am talking about the likes of those who roam the streets of Delhi wearing the hat of an event manager. They walk up to our office with a client in their kitty, then we execute everything for them, from the nail to the elephant at times, but in real life, they are bloodsucking vampires. Let me describe this particular one because, honestly, I have never met such a ruthless person in my life, and I hope God does not create any more of them. I have encountered people who are a bit like her but never the whole package, which she was.

I had known her for a few years by then and was sick of doing favours for her. It was like staying silent about being abused. Well, that was my fault as I always went out of my way and did things for her just to maximize my business gains, but there is a code of conduct among thieves too. But not with this one; her own wedding took the cake.

She made us do all the flower arrangements for her wedding functions, the draping, and also dye the drapes to create themes for her mehndi ceremony and wedding? She was a business associate, she was working with a big event management company who was one of our clients, but eventually realized that the kind of favours I had to do far outweighed the business I was getting from her. That calculation blew me away. But I must admit, she is the most calculative person I have ever met. She knew how to wring the best out of everybody, just to create an asset for herself absolutely free.

The mean girl even made me pay for the generators I installed in her home though I did not even own one. After the wedding was over, I knew what would happen next. A kid, and again she would suck my blood like a leech, and she did. After a couple of years, she had a child and she insisted we go shopping just a couple of months ahead of her delivery.

I was terrified of that day. She kept calling and whining till I took her shopping at her place of choice. That day was an eye-opener for me. While strolling around the store, I saw she had a small diary in her hand which was open. On one side my name was written on the top with a list underneath and on the other side, another name was written with another list underneath.

Under my name were listed: cot, stroller, sterilizer, and a bloody breast pump! I was infuriated but I somehow took hold of myself and waited for her to come up with it.

While looking around in the store, she handed me the diary and said, 'Just see what all I have written under your name.'

And then walked away. I quickly turned the pages of the diary.

Holy cow! It was a detailed shopping list of what she was taking from whom, even goddamned nappies! What a parasite! She had collected everything in her life by being cunning and ruthless. And I cannot sleep at night if I owe somebody money.

During our shopping spree, she came back with blankets, cot supports, bibs, nappies and whatnot, and kept them on the counter. Then she asked the lady in the shop if they had strollers. I quickly said, 'You can take mine as my daughter is three now.' That way, I could get off buying her a stroller case. Little did I know that she would hound me for that.

So, we were standing at the counter and the bill started rolling out when she turned towards me and said, 'Hope you're carrying cash.' My face fell and I could not believe her words.

But after that, I could not believe *my* words. I said, 'Yeah, sure. Don't worry.'

After clearing the bill of thousands of rupees, we made our way out of the shop discussing by when *my* stroller should reach her house.

'Babe, make sure you send it or you will have to get me a new one, hahaha!' She laughed like a hyena.

When I was alone, I realized how wrong it was to let someone do this to me. I was ashamed of myself. This bullying had to stop. I finally took the biggest risk of all. I decided that no way was I parting with my baby's stroller and no way was I importing one for her. Not happening!

As expected, I did not have to call her. She called me the very next day.

'Hi, babe. How're you?'

I croaked that I was fine.

'So, darling. Hope you have done the needful?'

Implying whether I had sent the stroller for dry-cleaning. 'Sorry, what? I don't remember.'

'The stroller, dumbo.'

I was flabbergasted! Dumbo? She called me a dumbo? Actually, I was happy she did that; I realized how dumb I was being. Why was I scared? My work was good and, in any case, she was just an employee of a wedding company. Why should I be so scared of her?

All these thoughts were running across my brain while I held the phone to my ear. I said, 'Ah, the stroller. Actually, I won't be able to part with it.'

'*What*!' She yelled. 'Are you actually saying you are buying me a new one? Aww, you are so sweet, Ras.'

'No.'

There was a pause. 'What do you mean?'

'I mean what you heard. There is no stroller. I cannot part with this one and after all that shopping massacre, I cannot afford to get a new one for you.'

'Oh really,' she replied. 'How much is your pending amount, Ras?'

I shuddered. I could not imagine she would come to it so suddenly and so soon. 'I don't remember. Why don't you check with your accounts? And what are you trying to say? That you will tell your office to stop my payment because I didn't buy you a stroller?'

'Oh no. Are you nuts? Don't be silly. I will make sure that that's your full and final cheque from us for the rest of your career as a wedding designer for us, darling.'

I had to threaten her that I would go and tell everybody how much bribe she had taken from us on every project. I was turning into a tiger from a lamb and I was so proud. It felt so good to lash back at her. I told her that I also knew about all the poor vendors—the *tentwalas* and the others she had always exploited for personal gains. After this, I started shaking and could not catch my breath.

She said, 'All the best,' and abruptly hung up.

I sat and mulled over every word I had spoken. They gave me the courage and confidence to pick up the phone and directly call the office of that woman and speak to the owner. I only wanted to make the owner aware of my pending payments but she invited me over for coffee for a heart-to-heart talk. But I just wanted to talk shop over coffee and be over and done with it soonest.

Thankfully, the meeting went beautifully. The owner of that hugely successful event management company with whom we had tied up for a number of weddings was a righteous lady. That office rat could not stop our payment as we had delivered and I then realized it was never in her hands. I was scared all this while for no reason. My predicament reminded me of the Mountain Dew advertisement—'*Darr ke aage jeet hai* (there is victory beyond fear)'.

Over coffee, we discussed forthcoming projects, brainstormed ideas, and planned winter and summer wedding looks. I did not speak a word against that woman as I am not malicious. This landed me the next project with that company. No prizes for guessing who the project manager was from their side.

Phew! So much for not telling on her.

The project was a very talked-about and sought-after birthday of an heiress, the only child who was turning sweet sixteen. Since the call came from the boss of the mean girl, I could not say no and there was absolutely no reason I could give for not wanting to work with the event manager in question. So, I accepted it as a challenge and we took on the project.

The mean girl knew now it was better that we handled our respective domains and stayed out of each other's way as I was just one scream away from blowing her cover. I saw her a little mellowed but, holy cow, where had we landed ourselves!

Here is what happened. Designs as well as sketches were being made on a design software. Since it was a joint project, we were in and out of boss lady's office. A modern-day fairyland, a fashionista theme, a rock-star theme, and many more were being worked on. The big car was packed to the roof with sketches, Macs, linen, and artefacts which would be used for the presentation. The car was followed by a mini truck which carried dining table, chairs, and lights for mood lighting. We were supposed to reach the client's farmhouse two hours before and do the set-ups which the family would come to witness.

We were on schedule. No excitement, same old shit. We set it up beautifully. It was a horrible sunny afternoon and we were waiting for the sun to be merciful so we could start the lighting and snap our fingers and create magic, but to my horror, in walked the to-be birthday girl, along with that woman, earlier than the stipulated time.

I was surprised. 'Hi, what are you doing here?'

She said, 'I wanted to see if I should even bother coming in the evening. Like, is it even good enough for me to come back? Clearly, I hate what I'm seeing.'

I somehow managed to smile and said, 'Darling, we are not ready as yet.'

'Yeah, but nothing will change. What's not straight will be straightened but what else can you do? It's really bad. It's nothing, it has not one thing which I like.'

By now, I was imagining that I was wearing the *Scream* mask, shutting up her mouth with a duct tape, and opening her eyes by shaking her up so that she could see beyond being such a spoilt brat. The tantrums of a sixteen-year-old!

I found my voice coming back after all that flight of imagination and I said, 'Fine, do you want me to finish the set-up as we are only thirty minutes away from dusk when the shimmer and lights will make it come alive? If you really feel like this, it's no point. I will leave it and wrap it up. It's cool.'

'Yeah, there is no point.'

I was aghast. After all the goddamned expense on the set-up and the brainstorming in office, we came up with something magnificent, and here, this *Tyrannosaurus rex* was busy on a rampage. The Mean Evelyn, the project manager, let out a chuckle seeing me flustered and then got busy on her phone.

I thought I'd better call the parents after the brat left. So, I sat while my team packed up, equally shell-shocked. By the time we were packing, it was already getting dark when another car pulled in and out jumped the parents. They walked up to the mock set-up and I narrated what transpired.

The couple had a private tête-à-tête and the father immediately got glued to his phone, apparently coaxing his daughter to come and clarify why she did not inform them about what she had done. The father got off the phone and asked, 'Can you please show me the set-up?'

I told them it was not possible as it would take us at least an hour to set it up again. He said, 'Fine, we will come back in an hour.'

Suddenly, the lights came on and my half of the set-up started to shimmer and dazzle, which greatly impressed the parents because they were smiling and looking very pleased with what they saw.

The mother came to me and said, 'We have a plan. We will call her in the evening tomorrow and say we have another designer to set up for her as a second choice and this time, I will get her with me so that she doesn't turn up earlier here.'

These people! Who do they think they are? They feel that the person standing in front is a robot with no feelings. The mom asked, 'Hope you don't mind? You go now and send your team. I will say they are from another design company and if she likes it, you can execute it.'

'Ma'am, I won't be able to do that—impersonate someone else. I think we should say goodbye nicely and please find a good designer.'

'I'm sorry but I can't go against my daughter's wishes. If I do, she will go on a hunger strike and even burn herself with a hair straightener as she is very short-tempered. She is never ready to take no for an answer.'

The situation was grave, but it was a big chunk of business that I would lose, so I decided to give it another shot.

'Okay, we will give you a re-presentation but please do not ask me to fake my identity. If she likes it, it has to be purely under our brand name or you can hire someone else.'

It was decided that a re-shot of the set-up would be prepared for the next day.

When we arrived the next day, the core team was already there, retouching the look. We had significantly changed the lighting and added more sparkle and glitter to the existing set, and with the right play of lights, we had cleverly changed the look, though marginally. But to her, it would look very changed because she had seen it in the daytime.

Our plan was to play on her senses. We therefore put vanilla- and candy-scented diffusers at the entrance, which would hit her as soon as she entered, provided her nose was not as blocked as her brain. And voila! *T. rex* walked in, smelling strawberries, blueberries, and fresh doughnuts from the ovens which were being baked, along with cakes, behind the props at the entrance.

She came running to me and said, 'It was so awfully done yesterday! I'm so happy you changed it for me! I love it! I love it! Mom, Dad, please keep them!'

The parents looked at each other as if conveying *mission successful*!

Sweet bitters changed to sweet sixteen. Overnight!

Evelyn was stunned at the change of heart of the little Dino. As for us, it was yet another eventful day.

22

The Wedding Battlefield

Before closing the book, I must write about an October wedding in which the whole theme was based on the Bhagavadgita.

I still have no idea which part of the Gita is inspirational for a wedding, but chose to stick to the brief rather than question the client because at the end of the day, what excites me is turning my client's dreams into reality. The wedding venue had to be large as the props were much inspired from the battle of Kurukshetra. *Seriously?* Well, they were *already* putting the bride and the groom on the battlefield.

So much for romantic candles, which turned into giant fire-breathing cauldrons; so much for the pretty stands, which turned into spears decorated with flowers; so much for the table decor which resembled archery quivers with flowers and arrows flying out of them. The entrance was decorated with shields and swords. It indeed looked like a battlefield. All we needed was some bloodshed and mutilated soldiers. It looked stunning but still not appropriate for a wedding. Come on, did we really make this? I was astonished seeing our work.

The colours were bright gold and silver; just to make them soft, we added lots of florals around the shields, and the handles of the swords had posies and ribbons. The stage was a marvel. It was 36 metres long and looked like the chariot Arjun rode. We had moulded wrought-iron horses with white stretchable fabric pulled over them, after which the fabric took the shape of a horse. We lit the horses in amber, which made them look fiery, bold, and battle-ready.

There were two huge horses in the front with long reins tied to the chariot. The reins were actually ropes of exotic flowers. The chariot was bright gold and was embellished with stones in green, red, and blue. It was made of fibre and fitted with a burgundy velvet seat for the couple to sit on. The seat was fitted facing the audience rather than the horses. The chariot was on four big wheels in copper-brown colour. The backdrop to all of this was a curtain of flowers and it looked just out of this world. The entire venue had huge velvet umbrellas dotted all over the lawn with seating underneath for the guests. One of our best creations.

At about 5 p.m., it suddenly became dark and the lights were still not on. As usual, the great meteorological department of our country could give us a timely update. The last coats of paint and touch-ups, the linen over tables and chairs, the cushions on the sofas—everything was yet to be done. It was an open field. After all, you cannot put the battleground under a tent.

Then winds started howling loud and clear, and the leaves of the trees rustled frenetically. The winds raked up a huge dust

storm; their power and fury was relentless. The entire team started running helter-skelter, trying to hold on to the props which swayed from side to side despite their heavy weight. Suddenly, I saw the huge dome structure of the *vedi*—which was decked up with half a truck of roses—shaking. If it toppled, there was no way we could heave it back up again as it had been erected with the help of a forklift.

The roses which were on the top layer were flying off the dome. I immediately pulled as many men as I could to run towards the structure, my frail workers running towards the vedi then scattered themselves on every pillar—clutching it, hugging it, one even wrapped his legs around it. They ran here and there catching tablecloths in the air as the quivers had toppled and the cushions were all over the place.

It was impossible to stand with dust in our eyes, making visibility poor, and the storm's power was like that of a demon unleashing his fury. I could just see everything crashing—figurines, shields, props, glass—and falling off.

I could see a herd of people here, a herd of people there, but could not recognize anybody. I was feeling so disoriented by now that I just started to pray really, really hard. What else could I do? I saw a flying horse up in the air crossing over me. Was it God? It took me a few seconds to realize what just happened and so I started running towards the stage.

Oh my god! The horses from my stage had flown away and the chariot had toppled just like in a battlefield. It had indeed become Kurukshetra. So much for evoking the spirits of war! What else will happen? Now what will happen? The wheels of the chariot were off. It was a total mess. Nothing could salvage the situation except a miracle. I could hear people screaming from a distance and I blindly ran in that direction and noticed that the vedi had turned into the Leaning Tower of Pisa.

Then, out of nowhere, I was hit on my head with what I thought was a big rock. I grabbed it and saw that it was a huge piece of ice. And then the hailstorm started. Big pieces of ice hit the ground with utter rage and violence. Somewhere, someone shrieked. I again started running towards the sound and it came from the spot where the bride's family was huddled. The dust storm started settling but the hailstorm was raging.

I quickly got them under one large umbrella which was being held by my men and tears were rolling down their cheeks. I wanted to say it was the fault of the theme, but all I heard myself say was, 'Don't worry. It will stop soon and we will make it all okay.'

They saw the horses lying on the ground—one far left, one far right—with all the things toppled over. It was truly a scene from hell. It was dark as the gensets were turned off to evade the possibility of fire from short circuit.

The father of the bride spoke, 'We've never done anyone wrong, so why has this happened to us?'

What could I say except giving false consolations? The damage was done, everything was broken and wet, torn and tilted. In those twenty-five minutes, everything was destroyed.

After the hailstorm stopped, I told my workers to set the vedi straight. Whether the guests would eat or not, whether the bride and groom would sit on a stage or not, *the wedding had to take place*. With this promise to the family and armed with my men, we headed straight to the vedi area and a hundred people got on to using their sheer physical strength to straighten the vedi without any machines. The sound of human power roared loudly and the impossible was made possible. We cannot win against nature's fury, but nature could not stop the bride from being duly married.

The *pheras* took place, the *jaimala* happened, the caterer managed to somehow serve something, hundreds of people could not turn up for the wedding because all over Delhi, trees had fallen and the traffic jams kept them away, which was great.

The few 100–200 guests who were there managed to finish the ceremony and, thanking us profusely, left for the Maurya Sheraton where they were staying. It was almost midnight when I was walking with my team in the battlefield where all my props lay like slain soldiers.

Never ever should this be the wedding theme where we evoked the spirits of the slain soldiers in Kurukshetra. Eerie ... very eerie.

Acknowledgements

I have to thank several good souls who held my hand when I took my first baby steps into the world of weddings.

First and foremost is God Almighty with whose blessings I embarked upon this quest.

Yash, my partner in life and crime, for always being my rock, for holding the ladder I climbed on, for putting my dreams ahead of his. He taught me what love is. Our daughter, Shailaja, the best baby traveller. Sometimes I feel guilty for the rough childhood, for the sunburn, and lost shoes but these adventures have made her rough and tough for life. My immense gratitude to her for understanding and cooperating with my hectic life. Even when she had not started talking, she would tell me with her eyes, 'Go on, mum, I'll be fine.'

Dad, a powerhouse of medical knowledge and a state-level boxing champion, for teaching me how to take life's punches and remain. I loved his attitude of 'So what, yaar'. Just these words made me feel silly about fussing over minor hiccups of life.

My grandmother, who was my partner in crime and had to double up as a mother to me and my little sister. She brought us up since we were teenagers and taught us how to be resilient. My mother—I hold your memories and try to master the balancing act, like you did. I miss you three every day.

My sister, Kanika, for just being there for me always. I love you.

Anupam, Karan, Atul, Jill, and Dean Anecki, thank you for your continuous encouragement to write this book. Neeti for literally dialling my literary agent's number, and putting the phone to my ear. I seriously owe this to her. Ashish Pandey for reminding me of some anecdotes I had forgotten.

My *vaanar sena*—each one uniquely talented and irreplaceable. Without these hard-working, never-say-die, courageous guys, I would still be building castles in air.

Mahadev, my florist, whom I call Edward Scissorhands. Shafiq, my welder, straight from a *Transformers* movie; he can create just about anything—car, dinosaur, or Eiffel Tower. Munna, my carpenter but a singer by heart. When he stops singing, it means he has slept. Sundar Chacha, our electrician, who can effortlessly walk the whole periphery of farmhouses connecting the wiring; if I could do that for even half an hour, I will consider myself fit to sprint in the Olympics. Ram Babu, who stitches a million cushion covers overnight like Speedy Gonzales. I still wonder how he does it. Last but not the least, my *karigars*, cooks, and craftsmen with whom I have shared many meals and many celebrations. Rajesh, my flower supplier, the Flying Jat who defies time, distance, and weather just to deliver my order, even if it is interstate and last-minute. I have no clue how he does it, but he has never let me down.

To my amazing team of tireless and restless souls, who never gave up, be it thunder, rain, cold, or blistering heat.

I remember when the shoes melted in the desert of Osian in Rajasthan, these guys did not let it get in their way. They wrapped T-shirts around their feet and continued working.

Kedar, my artist, who can expertly convert my abstract thoughts to reality. Many thanks to him for withstanding my many tantrums patiently and smilingly as I made him edit every design several times.

Kanchan, the small wonder, cute-as-a-button, little circuit board of energy, and brimming with so much goodness. I love her for her never-say-never attitude, and her inappropriate and hilarious statements when she gets all worked up have us in splits.

Babu, the multifaceted artist and production designer who could convert a haunted house into a palace, is now a successful art director in the Telugu film industry. He is an exceptional artist with a beautiful mind. We had a great run together; he taught me how to dance and I taught him how to drink, which made us an A-team.

Ms Meenakshi Mayor, whose faith allowed my dreams to become a reality. A huge thanks to her for giving me my first break, and for all the love and sunshine.

Ms Vinita Kochhar, my supporter, upholder, and believer. She has been a godsend angel and a friend. Her endorsement of my work propelled my career.

Vandana Mohan of the Wedding Design Company, by far the *best* wedding planner and designer the Indian wedding industry has ever seen. And my mentor.

Marion Marcatto, author, book reviewer, speaker, and teacher for reading my manuscript sitting on the other side of the world. And uttering these magical words that I hold so dearly: 'Your writing has the power to take the reader right into the action ... don't stop writing.'

Finally, none of this would have ever happened had it not been for Suhail Mathur, my literary agent, the dynamic and witty 007. I owe him deeply for his tireless guidance. My heart will always be full of gratitude for him and his team at the BookBakers.

My publisher, Ajay Mago, and chief editor of Om Books International, Shantanu Ray Chaudhuri, for bestowing their faith in me and my stories.

K.K. Malhotra, president of ITC Hotels, for sharing his mantra in life to work hard and party harder. This became our motto too and work became a lifelong party for Yash and me. He will always be remembered as we try to follow his robust, and positive, attitude to live life by making every day count.

I owe a deep gratitude to all my amazing clients who trusted me and made me a part of their celebrations.

To Mighty and MJ, my Great Danes, and Vucchy, my Labrador, my stressbusters. They would take all my tiredness away when they would come running to me flapping their ears at the end of a long day. I miss you both.